Surrounded by lights, Zoe all but glowed up there onstage.

Her hair fell in a long, soft wave over her bare shoulder. He wanted to kiss that shoulder. And her neck. Her mouth. Her nose.

She played the crowd like a pro, but her eyes returned to him time and again. He smiled at her. And something in her eyes gave him pause. Tucker needed to put the brakes on. So what if he'd gotten used to having her—and her baby—around?

Then the song ended and the place erupted in cheers and whistles. The impromptu concert was over. Zoe Parker was the new princess of the Nashville country music scene.

Zoe and the band disappeared backstage. Tucker followed. He stood back, observing. Zoe, surrounded by people, positively glowed. She looked up and her gaze fell on him. Her face lit up like a Christmas tree and suddenly she was flying toward him. She leaped. He caught her. And then their mouths clashed.

* * *

Billionaire Country is part of Harlequin Desire's bestselling series, Billionaires and Babies: Powerful men...wrapped around their babies' little fingers.

Dear Reader,

I grew up with country music. I rebelled a little in my teens and went rock-and-roll, though my all-time favorite artists were the storytellers—balladeers like Neil Diamond and Gordon Lightfoot. I also grew up with a dad who took me on a yearly road trip. Just the two of us. The biggest one we took was when he drove me to college. It was a weeklong journey of dad and daughter. One of the places we stopped was Nashville. Due to an ill-placed one-way street, and being typical tourists, we ended up at the back door of the Ryman Auditorium—home to the original Grand Ole Opry. A very kind security guard let us in and I walked out to stand in the middle of the stage. I did *not* burst into song. I don't sing. Stay with me, because this is going somewhere.

See, even though I'm not a singer and piano, guitar and bagpipe lessons were total failures, I love music. Listening, anyway. As a writer, I often find inspiration from songs. And last summer, I celebrated thirty-five years with my best friend and love of my life. In the slow cooker that is my writer's brain, these events all came together and culminated in *Billionaire Country*. Country music, road trips and finding the right one. I hope you'll come along for Tucker and Zoe's ride. Who calls shotgun?

Happy reading,

Silver James

SILVER JAMES

BILLIONAIRE COUNTRY

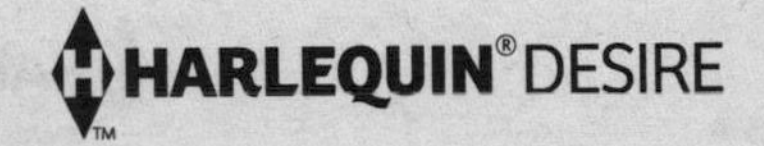

ISBN-13: 978-1-335-60351-7

Billionaire Country

This edition published by arrangement with Harlequin Books S.A.

For questions and comments about the quality of this book, please contact us at CustomerService@Harlequin.com.

Printed in U.S.A.

Silver James likes walks on the wild side and coffee. Okay. She LOVES coffee. A cowgirl at heart, she's been an army officer's wife and mom, and worked in the legal field, fire service and law enforcement. Now retired from the real world, she lives in Oklahoma, spending her days writing with the assistance of two Newfoundlands, the cat who rules them all and the characters living in her imagination.

Books by Silver James

Harlequin Desire

Red Dirt Royalty

Cowgirls Don't Cry
The Cowgirl's Little Secret
The Boss and His Cowgirl
Convenient Cowgirl Bride
Redeemed by the Cowgirl
Claiming the Cowgirl's Baby
The Cowboy's Christmas Proposition
Billionaire Country

Visit her Author Profile page at Harlequin.com, or silverjames.com, for more titles.

To best friends,
families and dreams that come true.
Many thanks to Charles, my editor,
who challenges me every step of the way,
all so my own dream can come true.
And with special thanks to Denise,
with the Metropolitan Nashville Department
of Communications, and the Nashville Police
Department for service above and beyond
when it came to dumb questions.
Thank you for all you do!

One

Tucker Tate was a man who knew where he was going. His life was exactly on track—and precisely where he wanted it. As the chief operating officer of Barron Entertainment, that life was never boring. The sun was shining, and he was tooling down Life's Highway in a vintage T-Bird, top down, wind in his face, radio cranked loud. He was single and free of familial duties, thanks in part to his brother Deacon getting married and adopting a baby, causing his mother to tone down the marriage rhetoric where her other six sons were concerned. Thank goodness! His cousin, and boss, Chase Barron, had also jumped onto the happily married-go-round, turning more of the business side over to Tucker. Which brought him to this glorious spring day.

He'd driven to eastern Tennessee from Nashville to check out a band performing at an amusement park with an eye to offering them a recording contract with Bent Star, the record company owned by Barron Entertainment. He had their demo tape and was leaning toward signing them, though he wanted one of the producers at Bent Star Records to take a listen. At the moment, he just wanted to enjoy a day of freedom. He'd opted to drive the long way home—heading to Gatlinburg for lunch before meandering through the Smoky Mountains as he headed vaguely north and west.

He didn't spend much time in the country. He appreciated his suite at the Crown Casino in Las Vegas and the company's luxury town house in Nashville's West End district. When he had to be home in Oklahoma, he stayed at the family ranch—mostly for holidays and the few command performances decreed by his mom.

The sun still hung high as Tucker drove toward I-40, taking every back road he could find. He passed a small country church perched on a low rise just off the road. A dirt and gravel drive led up to it and the clapboard building was surrounded by a variety of trucks and cars, some so beat-up he wondered that they still ran while others were tricked out enough to be show cars. As it was Saturday and there appeared to be an abundance of paper flowers and streamers on the vehicles, he figured a wedding was taking place.

It was a good day for a wedding, he decided—so long as it wasn't his neck in the noose. Marriage and kids were the very last thing on his mind. He was enjoying the heck out of his life.

Shifting gears, he took a curve in the road a little faster than was smart. He wasn't expecting the car charging up his six.

Jerking the wheel, Tucker cursed and fought gravity but kept the T-Bird between the lines. He blinked at the car that passed then pulled away from him. Was that a Trans Am? He laughed out loud. It was. It was a freaking *Smokey and the Bandit* Trans Am. Covered in paper flowers and trailing cans. *Good grief.* Then something white and filmy flew up through the Trans Am's open T-tops. He watched, fascinated, as the backwash from the car sent the thing soaring. Tucker slowed and downshifted, paying more attention to the material sailing toward him than the road.

A truck hit its air horn, and for the second time, Tucker jerked his car back into the correct lane—just in time for the white material to snag on his radio antenna. He slowed further, reached over and grabbed the lacy thing. It wasn't until he had it in his hand that he realized it was a wedding veil. Complete with a glittering tiara. Yeah, that gathering had definitely been a wedding, and evidently the newlyweds were in a real hurry to start the honeymoon. He accelerated back to the speed limit and wondered if the groom had the bride in his lap while he was driving, then hoped they wouldn't wreck.

Twenty minutes later, he spotted a cloud of smoke just over the crest of a hill. *Crap.* He hoped his wayward thoughts hadn't jinxed the couple. Tucker slowed down as he hit the hilltop. Halfway down, the Trans Am was pulled off to the side of the road. Oily black smoke poured from the exhaust pipes, but he didn't see any flames. The thing had probably blown its engine. As he edged his car closer, he caught sight of a woman wearing a white dress. She had the frothy skirt hiked up around her thighs as she kicked the car with her white Western boots. She glanced up—briefly—then went back to kicking.

Tucker pulled over and parked in front of the Trans Am. He looked around for the groom, but it appeared the bride was alone. *Curious.* He got out, and as her curses washed over him, he approached with a bit of trepidation. Apparently, the woman was not happy with the entire male gender. Taking his life and manhood in his hands, he stopped out of kicking distance.

What had she ever done to deserve all this bad karma?

Zoe kicked the Trans Am's door and enjoyed the boot-sized dent she inflicted. Movement flickered in the corner of her eye and she panicked. Once the Smithees figured out she'd run away, she was hosed. She rubbed her side.

"It's all gonna be fine," she murmured. "Momma's gonna fix everything." All she had to do was figure out how. The thought of that family getting their hands on her child sent ice water through her veins. They'd kept her a virtual prisoner until today. Seeing the Trans Am outside the church window and knowing she had a set of keys? She'd climbed out that window and run.

Zoe huffed out a breath when she recognized the classic black T-Bird with its lone male driver rolling her way. She started to raise her hand, but something stopped her from flagging him down. When it came to men, her instincts were on the fritz.

She kicked the car again, her massive ball-gown skirt gathered up in her arms to give her boot easy access to the metal. Dad-blasted piece of junk. Bad enough she'd had to drive it after Redmond's incarceration but the idea that she'd take it to go on her honeymoon with his blockheaded brother…

Good grief but Norbert was a moron. And his mother? That woman terrified her. Etta Smithee would be the mother-in-law from hell. The old bag should be run over by a reindeer. Or better yet, a Mack truck! Why the Smithees thought she would willingly marry Norbert just because he was Redmond's brother and Redmond was the father—

Someone cleared his throat and Zoe jumped. She whirled to face the stranger she'd passed on the road. Oh, good lord, why was she being so sorely tested? This man was…gorgeous. He was tall—towering at least a foot over her. His dark hair was short, cropped almost like a soldier's but had way more style. He looked perfect, unlike the Smithee brothers and cousins. Who would be on her trail all too soon. She refocused her attention on the intruder. He had eyes the color of cornflowers, which were crinkled in amusement. And his mouth. She could kiss that mouth for days and never need to come up for air. In other words, he was trouble in spades as he stood there in those tight blue jeans that hugged him like a jealous lover.

"Having a little car trouble?"

"Ya think?" She snapped at him and didn't know what to do when he grinned. She clutched the layers of material closer to her body, like her wedding dress would protect her from his sexiness.

"I'm a man. We're masters of the understatement." He eyed the beast, his expression dubious. "Need a lift?"

"I'm fine."

"Uh-huh. Sugar, I think you blew the engine. This bird isn't going to fly anytime in the near future." He gave her the once-over and she felt—actually felt—his gaze touch her. She shivered inside. *Guydar. On the fritz*, she reminded herself sternly. She realized how she'd hitched the ball-gown skirt of the wedding dress up around her middle, which bared her legs.

The dude cleared his throat. "So, sugar, want me to call a tow truck for your car?"

"No." Technically, it wasn't her car. Red had left her the keys, told her to drive it. She didn't give a flip if it sat here on the edge of the road from now until the day after the end of the world. A thought hit her. Leaving it might slow down her pursuers. Before she could ponder that further, her would-be rescuer spoke again.

"Look, this is the back of beyond. Let me at least give you a lift to the next town."

"I'm not goin' to the next town. I'm headed to Nashville."

"Fancy that. So am I. I'll take you."

And that was the whole problem. She wanted him to take her. He was still looking her up and down, interest sparking in those too-blue-to-be-safe eyes of his, and dang if she wasn't checking him out in return and hoping for a caveman. *Ugh*. What was wrong with her?

"All the way to Nashville?" That would give her a big head start on the Smithees. Red was in prison down in Alabama. Norbert was his mother's son and the Smithee cousins all followed Etta's orders.

"All the way." He held up his phone, and his brows creased in a cute way that made her want to kiss his forehead. *Whoa, girl*, she chided herself. This whole Handsome Man Syndrome was what had landed her in this mess to begin with. "Huh. No bars. I'll call a wrecker when we hit civilization."

Zoe leaned in through the door and grabbed her duffel bag and guitar case. Everything she owned fit in both. "Fine. Let's go." She marched past him, skirts still bunched around her middle, and got jerked to a stop when he snagged her bag.

"I'll put these in the trunk. The T-Bird doesn't have a back seat."

While the man deposited all her worldly goods into the minuscule trunk, she stomped to the passenger side door and snorted when she saw her veil crumpled there. Bad karma. Definitely. Zoe stuffed the ugly thing onto the dashboard and did her best to maneuver into the seat.

"May I help?"

She startled and banged her shin on the car door. Dang but the man was sneaky. She'd need to remember that fact. "No, I'm good. Thanks kindly."

He stood back, arms folded across a chest that filled out his crisp button-down shirt as well as his butt did those jeans. He'd rolled the sleeves up to reveal tan forearms sprinkled with dark hair that glinted copper under the sun.

With much huffing and puffing, she squirmed her way into the tight fit. Between the hideous excuse for a wedding dress and everything else, she'd need a forklift to get her out of the darn thing.

She reached for the door to close it, but the guy beat her to it. He stuffed the trailing edges of her dress in around her and managed to shut the car door without catching any part of her skirt. "I'd tell you to buckle up, but that dress is a built-in airbag."

"Ha ha, funny," she groused, pushing part of the tulle and netting down and tucking it around her legs. First gas station they came to, she was ditching this virginal white travesty and getting comfortable. With effort, she fought to stretch the seat belt over the material and got it fastened.

Moments later, he was settled behind the wheel. "I'm Tucker," he said, holding out his hand.

"Zoe." She eyed his hand while weighing the risk of touching him. Her palm all but itched to feel his skin. She gave in to temptation and they shook. His palm was warm and dry. But those were *not* little tingles racing up her arm. *Nope. Definitely not.*

"Should I ask where the groom is?" He gave her a sideways glance as he started the T-Bird. And didn't that sweet engine purr pretty? He pulled out onto the rural highway.

"Nope. Let's just say our nuptials weren't meant to be." She grabbed the veil and tossed it over her head.

She watched it through the side mirror and laughed when it draped across the firebird graphic on the hood of the Trans Am.

He cut his eyes her direction for a moment. "Cold feet?"

"Good sense." She flashed what she hoped was a reassuring smile in his direction.

"Okay." He dragged the syllables out.

She smoothed down her dress even more, grimacing at the miles of material. "You wouldn't happen to have some scissors? Or maybe a knife or something sharp?" The man—Tucker—glanced her way again so she explained, fluffing up the copious amount of material in her lap. "I want to cut some of the superfluous crap off this thing."

"No, sorry. Nothing that would work on that dress."

Zoe wanted to explain she hadn't picked out the dress, like this guy would care about her tastes in clothing. Still, she wanted him to think well of her. They rode in silence as miles passed. Fidgeting, she said, "You aren't from around here."

Tucker grinned. "Oklahoma originally. You?"

"Smoky Mountains, mostly, but I'm ready to get out and never look back." That was the truth. She sighed, wishing she'd dug her sunglasses out of her bag, and added under her breath, "One of the biggest mistakes I ever made was goin' to Gatlinburg to sing at that bar."

She glanced at Tucker, who was still watching her from the corner of his eye. She wanted to bite her tongue. Zoe knew exactly the picture she presented, and this guy had money and class stamped all over him.

"So you're a singer?"

Zoe hid her discomfort with a shrug. "Yeah, I am. And some days—" she tossed him her cheekiest grin "—I even get paid for it."

Zoe smooshed down some of the skirt between her thighs and squiggled her legs, still attempting to get comfortable. The silence returned. After several minutes, she glanced over at Tucker. He was casting surreptitious looks her way—only he wasn't checking out her face. Nope. He'd finally noticed her rounded belly.

Tucker cleared his throat, opened his mouth to speak, and evidently thought better of it because his jaw clamped shut. Zoe decided silence wasn't so bad. The man lasted all of five minutes.

"So, it was a shotgun wedding?"

"You could say that. Only it was my head they were holdin' the gun to."

He slammed on the brakes and her hands flew to the dash to brace her body. "What? What's wrong?" She swung her head back and forth looking for whatever emergency caused him to stop.

"Sorry! Sorry," he repeated, swiveling in the driver's seat to face her. "Please tell me that was…a euphemism. Or a joke. Or something."

"I wish I was jokin'." He scowled at her. "Hey, I didn't plan on my life takin' this detour." She shrugged. "I will admit, however, t'bein' young and dumb at the time."

"And now?"

"Older and wiser. Gettin' ready to have a kid and

watchin' my life turn into a bad soap opera will do that to a body."

Tucker glanced at her rounded belly. "Yeah? And you figured all this out when? All of...what, eight months ago?"

"About that." Zoe pressed her lips together, wondering how far she could trust this stranger. "My life is a tad crazy, Tucker. I figure the best I can do is grin and bear it. You know, laughter bein' the best medicine and all?"

"Don't you have family to help?"

She curled her lips between her teeth and bit down. Her eyes burned, and she looked away so he wouldn't see. The compassion she saw in his expression was about to undo her. "Don't have any family t'speak of. There's just me."

"I...wow." He looked surprised. "I can't imagine what that would be like. I have a huge family."

A big family? There'd only been Zoe and her dad. "Lucky you."

His smile was warm and fond. "Until they get all up in my business."

Zoe felt a sharp twinge. Grimacing, she pressed her palm against her side.

"You okay?"

"Yeah, it's just those Briggs & Stratton things."

He looked confused, opened his mouth to speak, then pressed his lips together for a moment. He eventually asked, "Don't you mean Braxton Hicks?"

Eyes twinkling, she tilted her head, pretending to

think about it, because of that whole laughter-being-the-best-medicine thing. She went for the cheap laugh. "Braxton Hicks. Doesn't he sing at the Grand Ole Opry?"

Two

Tucker hadn't missed the sheen of moisture in her eyes or her attempt at humor. From the white cowgirl boots to the froth of tulle and lace, she looked like a refugee from a hillbilly comedy show, but in her case, the clothing didn't define the woman hiding behind the caricature. In their short time together, he'd seen determination, warmth and an effervescent spirit. He admired the first and as a man, could appreciate the rest. He also sensed she was far more lonely than she wanted anyone to know. Given her circumstances? Totally understandable. He decided to play along. For now. "Ah, no," he said, hiding a grin. "Braxton Hicks are like false labor."

"No, really?" she said dryly, giving an exaggerated roll of her eyes. A moment later, she tilted her head to study him from under creased eyebrows. "How would a man like you know somethin' like that? You married?" He caught her checking out his left hand where it lightly gripped the steering wheel.

Biting back a bark of laughter, Tucker shook his head. Settling down was the last thing on his mind. "Nope. But that big family I mentioned? I have brothers and cousins. Some are married with kids." And his cousin-in-law Jolie, a nurse, had schooled everyone on the stages of pregnancy and birth when his Barron cousin Kade and wife, Pippa, went through the process. His gaze strayed to Zoe's belly again. Her hands were laced over it and he found the gesture…sweet.

Tuck eased off the brake, realizing he'd stopped in the middle of the road. Good thing there wasn't any traffic. "So tell me something." He glanced at her, waiting until she faced him to continue. "Were you serious about it being a shotgun wedding?"

An expression he couldn't immediately decipher flickered across her face. She shifted to stare out her side of the car, and he thought she'd ignore his question. Then he heard her sigh.

"That there would be a very long story. Are you sure you wanna wade around in my can of worms?"

And that there was a good question, he mused. By stopping and picking her up, he'd dived headfirst into her mess, and to be honest, his curiosity was getting the better of him. "It's a long drive to Nashville. We've got time."

"Well, sir, you've asked for it. Question becomes, where should I start?"

"The beginning always works for me."

"True, that. So…about nine months ago, I was singing my way from honky-tonk to roadhouse, and one night, I was fillin' in as a singer for the house band at Shooter Jake's." She looked his way to see if he was following along. "You've heard of it?"

He nodded. Shooter Jake's, in Dalton, Georgia, was one step up from a roadhouse, but the owner had an ear for music and a willingness to give talented newcomers a chance. He wasn't going to admit precisely how familiar he was with the place. It had been Jake himself who put Tuck on the trail of the band he'd just auditioned.

"So anyway, it was a one-night deal. Their lead singer came down with something and couldn't perform. Mr. Jake introduced me to 'em—the band, I mean. Come dark, there I was, front'n center on the stage."

"Okay?" He wondered if maybe one of the band members was responsible for her current condition.

"That night I was singin' my heart out and there was a guy sittin' there at a table. He was downright good-lookin', if you know what I mean?" She cut her eyes toward him and winked. "Not as handsome as you, but dang close. Anyway, he bought me a drink. And then another. And so on, until…well, you get my drift." She paused and waggled her finger in his direction. "Now, I might not be a good girl, but I ain't normally stupid, even if I've drunk way more whiskey than is good for me. We took precautions but…" She sighed. "Sometimes, stuff happens. Come mornin', he went his way while I went mine."

"Uh-huh." Tucker was fascinated, despite his better judgment.

"Well, due to circumstances…" She patted her belly. "That stuff happened. I bought a test to confirm it."

Tucker had the insane urge to touch her belly. "It was obviously positive."

"Yup. So, I went lookin' for the man. I figured he had the right to know, seein' as he was the daddy and all." She glanced over at him. "I mean, wouldn't you want to know?"

He considered the question. "Yes, I would."

"Took me two months to track Redmond down, and by then, it was a little late to be doin' anything about the situation." Her chin rose in a stubborn jut. "Not that I would have, even if that's what he wanted. That solution is fine for some people, but not me." She rubbed her belly with one hand, a gesture both protective and soothing, and one Tucker thought she was unaware of. He found it…endearing.

"So…" Tuck stretched out the word. "You wanted him to marry you?"

"Oh, hell no! I mean really, it's not like love had a thing to do with it." She inhaled deeply and breathed out slowly. "And I wasn't out to trap him. I'm not that kind of woman."

Given that she was running away from her wedding, obviously not. Tucker said as much. "Since you're here with me and not on your honeymoon, I sort of figured that."

Zoe blinked rapidly at him. "I told you my life has turned into a soap opera. Are you sure you want to know all this?"

At his nod, she continued. "I didn't discover until too late that I shoulda just hightailed it outta there. Redmond let on that he was prouder than a bantam rooster about bein' a daddy, but did he take care of me or help with doctor bills? Nope. That sonavagun dragged me all over the South, stallin' every step of the way." She dropped her voice as she mimicked. "Just one more job, baby girl, then I'll give you some money." She rolled her eyes and grimaced. "I plead pregnancy hormones because if I'd been in my right mind, I would have ditched that man way before I did."

"Uh-huh." He didn't hide the dubious tone in his voice.

"Trust me, I'm serious. Anyway, we were down in Tuscaloosa, Alabama." She started to say more but caught herself. "Let's just say things went downhill. He turned out to be a...well, Redmond liked the ladies. A lot. And it got him in a whole heap of trouble."

Tucker didn't like the way her voice sounded. "What kind of trouble?"

"Unbeknownst to me, he took up with another man's wife. And got caught with his britches down. T'make a long and sordid story short, there was a shoot-out. Red walked away. The husband didn't."

She heaved out a sigh and rubbed her side. Tucker waited, silent now. This was quite a tale, but he felt the urge to reach over and take her hand, to tell her that everything would be okay.

"I was ready to take off as soon as he was arrested, but Etta Smithee, his momma, had different ideas. She made me stay in Tuscaloosa for the duration. Sat me down in the front row, right there behind her baby boy every day of that trial. She bought me all these frilly maternity clothes and there I sat, day after day, lookin' and feelin' like a fool. I didn't love that man, and he deserved to be sent to prison for killin' that boy."

"I…" Tucker paused. What could he say?

She favored him with a sidelong but understanding look before continuing. "As soon as the jury read the verdict, I was ready to hit the road. Before I could go, Miz Smithee got all sweet, sayin' it was up to her and the Smithee family to look after me and the baby. Things were fine until she decided to make an honest woman of me. Since I wouldn't marry Red, I'd just have to marry Norbert, his brother." She issued a long-suffering sigh. "Mama Smithee wants all her chicks in a row and all her loose ends tied up. And those loose ends would be me and Baby Bugtussle here."

Tucker tried to wrap his brain around this information, failed and gave up. "Why would she want you married to Norbert?"

"That woman is covered in crazy sauce. She decreed that her first grandbaby should have the Smithee name, and I should just be dancin' with joy to marry Norbert. Like any smart woman, I hitched up my skirts and hightailed it out of town first opportunity I got. I went back to singing and was doin' pretty good despite the extra baggage." She patted her belly, a big smile curling up the corners of her mouth—a mouth Tucker found most intriguing. "I got a job in Gatlinburg. I had no idea the Smithees roosted around there. There I am, strummin' my guitar and singin' a Miranda Lambert song and who walks in the door?"

"Norbert."

"Got it in one, slick." She winked at him, but her smile faded and a haunted look filled her eyes. Tucker tensed, not sure he wanted to hear the rest. "Next thing I know, he's stuffin' me in his old truck and drivin' like a bat outta hell straight to his momma's house. That woman locked me up in a bedroom until she could—" Zoe paused and formed air quotes with her fingers. "Make arrangements."

"Did those arrangements include that…dress?" He wanted to banish the ghosts lingering in her eyes so he tried her trick of making a joke.

"Absolutely." She squirmed a little and sighed. "Speakin' of, got any idea how far it is to the next gas station so I can change clothes? And…" She pressed her side and stiffened a little. "This little sucker just loves stompin' on my bladder. I could use a rest stop." She blew out a breath. "Sooner than later."

Tucker couldn't decide how much of Zoe's tale was fact and how much was fiction. He had to admire what his mom would call gumption. She was all alone and he caught a hint of the distress she tried so hard to hide. She was sweet and funny and he wanted to protect her, as inexplicable as that seemed, considering they'd just met. He resisted reaching for her hand. Again.

In the back of his mind, a thought formed—he should have his brother, Bridger, who worked for their cousin Cash Barron at Barron Security Services, look into the Smithees. Out loud, he said, “I think I can manage to fulfill that request.”

Zoe stashed the hated wedding dress in the dumpster behind the truck stop and finally felt like herself. Struggling out of the darn thing, even in the handicapped stall, had been an exercise in futility. Surrendering, she just ripped at it until all the buttons popped, pinging off the metal walls like BBs. The tussle left her dizzy, and she had to sit on the commode and gather herself for a moment before she could pull on yoga pants. Topping them with an oversize T-shirt and slipping her swollen feet into flip-flops was pure indulgence. The hideous dress had been gag inducing. The cheap boots followed the dress into the trash.

Grabbing her duffel, Zoe schlepped back toward the store portion of the truck stop. She had just enough cash to grab something cold to drink and maybe a sandwich. She’d locate Tucker and then they could hit the road again. She reached the back door but hesitated to open it, opting instead to peer through the glass. She froze. Two Smithee cousins stood in the checkout line. Could Etta Smithee be far behind?

She ducked away from the door. Pressing her back against the sun-warmed concrete wall, Zoe breathed through the panic. She couldn’t go inside to grab Tucker. *What to do? What to do? Think, think, think.* She needed her guitar. Which was locked in the trunk of Tucker’s car. She shifted just enough to peek through the glass door. The cousins were still there but there was no sign of Tucker.

Edging along the wall to the corner of the building, Zoe checked the busy parking lot. Tucker had parked away from everyone else. That was a good thing. The T-Bird couldn't be seen from inside the store. She located a rust-bucket pickup she'd seen parked at the church. The truck was empty. The minute those two saw her, the jig would be up, but if Tucker would come out, they could escape unnoticed. She was running out of time and options. Fast.

Zoe glanced at the big semis idling in the truck lot. Maybe she could hitch a ride. But that meant leaving her guitar behind. And Tucker. Leaving him behind didn't seem like much of a solution. Which was dumb because that man owed her nothing and would probably turn her over to Etta and Norbert just on principle. Too bad he was so pretty. And manly. And made her think of things no woman within a month or so of giving birth should be considering.

But Zoe didn't truly believe Tucker would hand her over to the Smithees. That meant she had only one option. Wait for Tucker. Sneaking over to the T-Bird without looking like she was skulking through the parking lot wasn't all that easy. Worried other Smithees might be around, she ducked down on the driver's side of the classic car. Too bad it was so low-slung. Sexy, yes, but dang hard to hide behind.

"C'mon," she murmured, sending vibes winging toward Tucker—not that she believed in any of that woo-woo stuff. But five minutes later, her headache-inducing concentration worked. Tucker, holding a plastic bag, stepped out of the store and looked toward where he'd parked the T-Bird. Zoe watched his brow knit as he glanced back inside. That was her cue. She popped her head up, put two fingers in her mouth and issued a piercing whistle. His head jerked back toward her and she waved him over, her arm flailing, as she climbed in.

As he walked up to the passenger door—the side of the car nearest the store, she pleaded, "I need the keys." She gripped the steering wheel with white-knuckled strength so Tucker wouldn't see how badly her hands shook. When he didn't respond fast enough, she added, "Get in. Please! We have to move fast."

He stared at her very pregnant belly crammed against the steering wheel and raised a brow. Okay, he might have a point as she tended to waddle when on foot, but she was driving, and they had a need for speed.

"How can you—"

"C'mon, rich boy. We gotta go and go now!"

The doors behind him opened and shouts echoed over the growls of idling diesel engines. Tucker glanced around, saw two men bearing down on them. He tossed the keys to Zoe and she managed to get the right one inserted into the ignition as Tucker vaulted into the passenger seat. Zoe floored the accelerator before he got settled. Thank goodness Tucker had backed into the parking space.

The men lumbered after them but gave up within a few yards, turned and trotted to their truck as Zoe watched through the rearview mirror.

"Pull over," Tucker ordered.

"Not until we lose them." She was adamant.

"Who are those guys?"

"They woulda been my in-laws, if I hadn't run like hell." She pressed back against the seat and fought the car around a tight curve, refusing to slow down. "Well, sort of. They're Norbert's cousins. Won't be long until Etta and him will be on our trail."

Tucker reached over, placing a hand over hers on the steering wheel. "I won't let them hurt you."

Her eyes filled with tears that she blamed on the wind, since she'd forgotten her sunglasses again. And she ignored the twinge in her chest where her heart beat in loud thumps. Tucker was just a nice man helping out a stranded woman in trouble. That's all. Nothing more. But no man had ever said those words to her and meant them. She didn't have to swipe at the tear on her cheek. Tucker did it for her with a gentle fingertip.

"We got this, sweetheart." He rummaged in her duffel and pulled out her sunglasses. Then he reached into his plastic bag. He gave her a wink and a grin. "Wouldn't be a road trip without junk food."

Three

Tucker let Zoe drive as she seemed to have some clue about their location. She didn't pop the clutch when she shifted gears, instinctively braked before hitting the curves, then powered through them by accelerating. The day was sunny, not too warm, and her not-quite-in-laws were way behind them. Besides, by not driving, he could study his runaway bride.

Zoe was pretty, though not in the beauty queen sense. Her eyes, hidden now behind big sunglasses, were a deep chocolate brown. Her chin was too long, her mouth too wide but not full and her nose tipped up on the end. Her long, dark brown hair fell in twisty—and hair-sprayed—curls down over her cleavage. There was just something wrong with him for thinking about her in any sort of sexual way, but he couldn't help himself. She wasn't the sort of woman he normally would be attracted to, yet he was. She exuded a sweet vulnerability that called to him.

Her accent was thick enough—and country enough—he could cut it with a knife. He had a Harvard MBA and remembered all too acutely the disdain he'd received there for his Okie accent. He'd worked hard to smooth out the rough edges. But Zoe? Her language was colorful and brash, and whenever she opened her mouth, the lyrics to a country song spilled out. Maybe that was why she fascinated him. Tucker continued to study her.

She had long, supple fingers—and didn't the idea of them gripping him like she had them wrapped around the steering wheel make him shift in his seat. They ended with short nails covered in chipped red polish. Her arms looked toned and he wondered what her figure was like before the pregnancy. He jerked his thoughts away from jumping down that rabbit hole.

She drove with a carefree abandon *and* a determined focus. She was a free spirit, not ready to settle in one place. Except she'd decided to keep the child of a man she claimed was a one-night stand she didn't wish to marry. Zoe was a paradox and his curiosity might just kill his cat. Good thing he didn't own one.

"You're staring."

"Yup."

"I need to pee again."

"Okay."

She cut her eyes his direction. "I'll be stoppin' at the next place we come to. You can drive after that."

"Gee, thanks," he said dryly. "Considering it's my car." He flashed her a mock glower and added, "Though I'll admit you're not a bad driver."

She made a *pfft* sound before she laughed. And, man, did her laughter arrow straight into his core. "Honey, I learned to drive when I was ten so I could borrow the neighbor's car. My daddy couldn't drive so I'd take us down to the local dive where I could play for my supper and his drinks."

This woman fascinated Tucker. And he worried about that, just a little. She was raw and…real. She said what she thought with no filters, and no matter how horrified he might be, he still found himself enjoying her company. In the back of his mind, though, resided that little voice of doubt. Was she telling a tall tale, or was this the truth of her life? He understood that not everyone had the '50s sitcom life he and his brothers had grown up with—a strong mother, a doting father, hard work but lots and lots of love, and parents who gave their boys the freedom to fly when they left the nest. All but his baby brother, Dillon. But that was okay. Between him and Deacon, they were keeping him in line.

Pulling his thoughts back to the woman driving his car, Tucker noticed Zoe was squirming in her seat. He surreptitiously searched the map app on his phone. "Can you last five more miles?"

Zoe glared at the speedometer then scowled as they passed a speed limit sign. The little car sped up. A lot. Tucker choked off a laugh. Less than five minutes later, she braked to a sliding stop at the travel mart just off

I-40. She got the stick shift in Neutral, heaved out of the seat and waddled inside. Zoe wore such a determined look on her face that men scrambled out of her way. Tucker waited until she was out of sight and then he burst out laughing. Several people walking past the T-Bird stared at him. He didn't care. He'd been totally charmed by his hitchhiker.

By the time Zoe returned, Tucker was sitting in the driver's seat. He started to get out to hold the door, but she waved him off.

"I may be as big as a small barn, but I'm not helpless. The day I can't open my own door, I'll be flat on my back in a coffin."

"Yes, ma'am, if you say so."

"Are you makin' fun of me?"

"No, ma'am. Not me."

She gave him a narrow-eyed scowl. He just managed to keep his face averted so she couldn't see the grin teasing his mouth. Too cute. Even pregnant with swollen ankles and a small bladder, she was too cute. "I'm taking the interstate so we're about two, two and a half hours from Nashville. You gonna need to stop again?"

"Your guess is as good as mine. It depends on Baby Bugtussle." She suddenly sat up straighter and blew out a slow breath. "Swear to the angels above this child is gonna be a placekicker for the University of Tennessee Volunteers."

Tucker glanced past her, watching traffic, before pulling out onto the highway. "Do you know what it is?"

"Etta Smithee is convinced it's a boy."

"You haven't had an ultrasound?"

"I've had three. The little dickens gives the camera its butt. Not one scan has shown this child's privates. If I had a nursery, I'd have to paint it lavender."

"Lavender?"

"Yup. Mix pink and blue. Makes lavender."

"How about green? That seems like a neutral color."

"Nope. Baby Bugtussle has done stepped on my last nerve. Gonna paint everything lavender. Then if it is a boy, he can just explain things to his friends."

"Why not just name him Sue?" Tucker muttered.

Zoe laughed and launched into a few measures of Johnny Cash's "A Boy Named Sue." She offered a raucous rendition of the song. The part of him always on the lookout for new talent picked up something in her voice, but she stopped singing before he got a handle on just what he heard. He realized her voice made him think of moonlight and rumpled sheets, of a man and a woman entwined in the dark. He liked the vision in his head—probably a little too much.

They didn't talk. At highway speed, the wind blew away their words. Zoe gathered her hair in one hand to keep it from whipping around her face. The silence wasn't uncomfortable, which surprised him. He caught himself watching her almost as much as he kept his eyes on the road. Her voice and laugh burrowed their way into him, as did the hint of uncertainty and sadness he sensed behind her good humor. The way her high cheeks complemented the line of her jaw, the curve of her throat as she arched her head back… She was far too attractive for his own good. He found himself lost in contemplating her face. Until he glanced down to the rounded bulk of her pregnant belly. That was like taking the ice bucket challenge every time.

They hit the outskirts of Nashville just over two hours later. Traffic thickened as they approached the east side. He needed to know where to drop her, so he asked. She took her time answering, and Tucker watched the lighthearted mask she hid behind slip a little. She finally asked to borrow his phone, only she didn't make any calls. Her thumbs flew over the screen as she texted someone. Then she waited, eyes glued to his phone.

When she didn't give him directions or an address, he took the exit for downtown Nashville and headed to the restored fire station that now housed Bent Star. His passenger looked up as the car rolled to a stop at Second Ave.

"Where are we?" Zoe's forehead crinkled as she gazed around.

"I'm headed to my office unless you have someplace else in mind?"

She tucked her chin and shook her head. "No. Not really. I texted a friend of mine, but he hasn't replied yet. I was going to camp out on his couch."

Tucker didn't like the idea of this male friend of hers. Which was ridiculous. Except he liked Zoe and was worried about her being stuck in Nashville all alone. He didn't say anything until he pulled into the parking lot at Bent Star and cut the T-Bird's engine. With both hands on the steering wheel, he slid his eyes her direction but didn't look at her full-on. "Do you have another place to stay, Zoe?" She lifted a shoulder, head still down. "I can take you to a hotel."

"I'm good," she insisted. "Don't put yourself out. I'll just head to my friend's." He watched her shoulders slump in a defensive move. "Can I get my stuff from the trunk?"

"Sure." He slipped out of the car and retrieved her guitar case and duffel. He carried both around to the passenger side and after watching her struggle for a long moment, set down the bag and extended his hand. "Here. For leverage," he added when she scowled at him. Once she was out of the car, she slung the straps of the duffel over her shoulder, handed him his phone and clutched her guitar case.

"Well, thanks for all the help and stuff. Sorry for getting you caught up in all my drama." She offered a wan smile, turned away and started walking.

Tucker glanced down at his phone and noticed a reply text. "Well, crap," he muttered. His mother would disown him if she ever found out he let a down-on-her-luck pregnant girl just walk off into the sunset. "Zoe!"

She kept walking, picking up speed when Tucker yelled her name. If she could get downtown, she might find one of the clubs with an open mic night where she could sing for tips or something. That would get her a room until she could reach the guy she'd hoped to stay with.

Pounding steps echoed behind her, then a warm hand settled on her shoulder, halting her.

"Your friend texted back." He held out his phone

so she could read it. "He's out of town, touring with a band." She closed her eyes to hide the tears prickling there. Just once she wished things could go her way. She felt wrung out, and so tired she hurt all over.

"You don't have any other place to go, do you?" Tucker's voice sounded full of compassion. She hated that he might pity her but before she could make up something, he continued. "And I'm betting you don't have much money, either." He tugged the duffel off her shoulder and hefted it over his own. Then he relieved her of the guitar case. "C'mon. I have a couple of things to take care of at the office. Then we'll go eat something and figure out things from there."

"Look, you don't—"

"Yeah, I do. I'm not going to just dump you out on the street, Zoe. I wasn't raised that way."

They walked back to the redbrick Victorian building. Once upon a time, it had been a firehouse. There was no sign to designate what sort of business occupied the space. Tucker hadn't mentioned what he did for a living. Given the expensive boots and the classic car he drove, he had money.

He held the front door for her and ushered her inside. He could do…almost anything. Lawyer. Real estate. Heck, this was Nashville. He could be in the music business. The reception area had a country-western feel with lots of leather furniture and barn wood with a logo shaped like a Texas Ranger's star behind the desk.

Tucker led her down a long hall that opened into another waiting area, still decorated in the same theme, only the artwork consisted of album covers and awards.

Agent, she decided. Tucker must be a music agent. Either he window-dressed a good story or he had some major clients, according to the stuff lining the walls.

"Have a seat. I'll be a little while," he said, then disappeared behind a closed door—with her guitar case and bag. She was too tired to object.

She wandered around the space, stretching her legs. The secretary's desk held only a phone console. She found the restroom and availed herself of it. As she wandered back to the sitting area, she noticed a worn acoustic guitar sitting on a stand. Unable to resist, she picked it up and settled in a large chair that could accommodate two people, if one of them wasn't pregnant.

Zoe curled up, as much as her belly allowed, on the wide padded seat. Using her thumb, she tested the tone of each string, listening intently. Surprised to find it in tune, she strummed a few chords. The old Gibson had an amazing sound. She riffed through a progression of chords, humming softly. Lost in the music, she didn't realize she had an audience.

She sang a Carrie Underwood song, then launched into a rollicking Miranda Lambert tune. She finished up with Kelly Clarkson's heartbreaking ballad, "Piece by Piece." Zoe didn't get to sing ballads often. Working the bars, the folks there wanted up-tempo dance tunes. But her soul found solace in the ballads, the songs like this one, or like Cam's "Burning House." She lay her cheek against the swell of the guitar and just let her hands wander along until they started picking the melody to Striking Matches' "When the Right One Comes Along." She raised her voice to sing, getting through the first stanza of the duet. She took a breath before starting the part where the male voice would harmonize, and almost dropped the guitar when a voice picked up where she'd left off.

Jerking her head up, she gaped at the five men standing there, but it was the singer who held her attention. He'd picked up the song on his own guitar and winked at her as he waited for her to catch up. Her voice found his pitch, and as she began to sing again, he altered his tone to match hers. Outwardly, she remained calm but inside? Inside she was squeeing like a fangirl sitting in the front row of this man's concert. Deacon Freaking Tate. Along with his band, the Sons of Nashville. She managed to get through the song, even adding some harmony from the guitar in her lap.

When they finished, the band applauded, but she was so flustered she couldn't speak. Was this what it felt like to be famous? Fame had been a pipe dream from the time her daddy had put that first pawnshop guitar in her hands.

Deacon walked up to her, a big smile on his face. She'd thought he was sexy on TV but in person he was off the charts. He held out his hand.

"Deacon Tate."

She sucked in a breath and thought, *Of course you are*. Then she introduced herself, placing her hand in his. "Zoe Parker."

"Nice to sing with you, Miss Zoe Parker."

"Trust me, the pleasure's all mine."

"Aren't you married?" a gruff voice barked from behind the band. "And doesn't your wife carry a gun?"

Deacon laughed, the sound as rich and lyrical as his singing voice. "Yes, and yes, Tuck. You didn't tell us you had such a talented lady waiting for you. We'd have finished sooner."

Zoe forgot to breathe as Tucker pushed through the cluster of band members and halted next to Deacon. Only then—with them side by side—did she recognize the similarity. "Are you… I don't…?" she sputtered.

"Zoe Parker, I'd like to introduce my brother, and the chief operating officer of Barron Entertainment, Tucker Tate," Deacon interrupted. He bumped Tucker with his shoulder, amusement lighting up his handsome face. "And there's no need to be jealous, little bro."

Her gaze darted between the two men for about five seconds as her brain roller-skated on a hamster wheel. Tucker Tate? He was like a gazillionaire. And important. Breath caught in her lungs. *No hyperventilating,* she ordered herself. Something twinged low in her back and the pain that had been building there all day exploded as her water broke.

Zoe looked up, horrified and embarrassed. The men stared at her, then at each other. She pressed her hand over her mouth as they erupted into shouted orders and pandemonium as everyone started running around shouting and flailing their arms.

"Call nine-one-one!"

"There's not time!"

"I'll get the car!"

"We need an ambulance!"

Then Tucker and Deacon were beside her, holding her up. "Shh, Zoe. It's okay," Tucker soothed.

She gazed into Tucker's face. He appeared only slightly panicked. "If you say so."

"I do. Just hang on." His arm slipped around her shoulders. "We got this, remember?"

And then the EMTs were there, bundling her onto a stretcher and moving her to the ambulance. They loaded her, and she saw Tucker standing outside, staring at her and looking as lost as she felt.

"C'mon, Dad," one EMT said, waving Tucker aboard. "I have the feeling the baby isn't going to wait for an invitation. You need to be close."

Tucker climbed in and moved to crouch on the bench near Zoe's head. The second EMT headed to the ambulance cab and in moments, they pulled out, lights blazing and sirens blaring.

"I'm Ted," the EMT said.

"Zoe."

"I need to take a peek, Zoe, to see where we are in the process. Okay?"

Tucker looked away as the EMT cut off her pants and checked. He gulped when the guy said, "Ah, darlin'? You need to stop pushing."

"Stop pushing?" Zoe yelled. "What in bloody blue blazes are you sayin'? This baby wants out!" She waved her left hand in Tucker's direction.

He grabbed it out of sheer instinct. She squeezed hard, grunted, then panted. She clutched his hand so tight, he lost feeling in his fingers. The EMT *tsked* a few times as he draped a thin cotton blanket over Zoe and fussed with getting monitoring equipment on her.

"I don't wanna do this," Zoe wailed.

"Little late for that, angel." Tucker smoothed a tangle of hair off her face and wondered what it would feel like once the hairspray was washed out. Her face was pinched from pain and her eyes were fixed on him. He tried to smile but he wasn't nearly as calm as he tried to project.

A low moan escaped from between lips pressed tightly together and her shoulders came off the stretcher. "Gotta push," she snarled between clenched teeth.

"Just hang on, little momma. We're almost there." Ted lifted the blanket to check her again, his gaze bouncing to the monitoring equipment.

"Aren't you supposed to be doing some breathing or something?" Tucker wanted to distract her. He got a growl and a light punch in the arm for his efforts.

"So not funny, you—" Whatever she meant to say was lost in another, more powerful groan.

"Speed it up!" Ted yelled toward the cab of the ambulance. The ambulance accelerated.

Tucker watched as the EMT muttered something and flipped the blanket up to Zoe's knees and positioned himself between her legs. Moments later, Ted said, "Looks like we're doing this anyway. Time to push, Zoe."

The contraction hit, and Zoe squeezed Tucker's hand again as she bore down. He slipped an arm under her shoulders and gave her support as she pushed.

It seemed like an hour before she went limp, leaning back into him as the EMT held something pink and squirming. Which then started screaming at earsplitting levels to rival the siren. Tucker barely had time to catch his breath before Ted was placing a naked bundle in Zoe's arms.

Tucker looked down at the tiny, scrunched-up face and felt his heart stop. He brushed a fingertip along the baby's cheek and the child stopped crying. Able to breathe again, he marveled at the tiny thing, all thick dark hair and blue eyes. Part of him was stunned but another part was full of awe, and some emotion he couldn't—nor did he want to—define. But his brain spun through the possibilities despite his best efforts. Protectiveness. A weird tenderness. Tucker figured in that moment that he was a goner. This kid would own him heart and soul if he didn't guard against it.

"Congrats, Mom and Dad. It's a boy."

Four

Tucker didn't have the presence of mind to correct the EMT. Zoe cradled the baby in her arms and stared at her child, teary-eyed, her expression filled with wonder. He glanced at his own expression, distorted as it was in the gleaming metal of the cabinet across from him. He and Zoe both looked like they'd been struck by lightning—dazed, confused and in awe of the tiny person who'd just made his grand entrance into the world.

Sitting here in an ambulance, amid the chaos of a birth, Tucker should have been totally freaked out. Except he wasn't. Maybe it was shock—because what he'd just seen couldn't be unseen—but at the same time, there was a deep sense of peace. *That's* what was turning him into a babbling idiot. Tucker clamped his teeth together to keep the babble in his head.

He concentrated on Zoe. She had no place to stay, no friends, no family. He should take care of her, but at the same time, he was a stranger and one with slightly ulterior motives, after hearing her sing. Tucker was well aware of all the scandals involving powerful men and the women with stars in their eyes those men exploited. He was *not* that guy. Never would be. But he couldn't deny his attraction to her, either.

The ride smoothed out as the frantic rush to the hospital wasn't quite so necessary now that the baby had arrived. The ambulance rolled to a stop, then backed into a slot beneath the covered parking at the entrance to Vanderbilt University Medical Center's emergency room. The back doors opened, and the paramedic's partner appeared, along with a trauma nurse and orderly. Bemused, Tucker watched as Zoe and her baby were unloaded.

"Yo, Dad! Ya comin'?" the paramedic called.

Shaking the cobwebs out of his head, Tuck clamored down and followed the little parade into the emergency department. No one stopped him, not even when he trailed after the gurney into a partitioned cubicle. When Zoe didn't chase him out, he settled onto a short "wheely" stool. A scarily efficient woman in scrubs covered with rainbow unicorns conferred with Zoe, tapping information onto an electronic tablet with a stylus. As she finished the intake, a man and a woman bustled in.

"OB-GYN and pediatrician," Unicorn Lady explained as she stepped out of their way. Tucker rolled back into the corner and pushed off the stool. Time for him to go. Before he could make an escape, questions flew fast and furious from the doctors and Unicorn Lady.

"Due date?"

"Blood pressure?"

"First child?"

"Apgar?"

Zoe ended up with her feet in stirrups, knees spread, while the mumbling OB-GYN ducked under the sheet a nurse had spread over Zoe. The male pediatrician bundled the baby up in a blanket. Tucker got two steps before Zoe grabbed his hand.

"Please?" Her breathy voice tugged at him just as hard as her hand did.

She looked scared and overwhelmed and totally alone. Tucker's protective instincts surged, and he gave her hand a gentle squeeze. "I'm not goin' anywhere, Zoe." The smile she flashed was radiant—and relieved. His breath clogged in his chest as he smiled back.

The pediatrician noticed him. "Congratulations. You have a healthy if slightly impatient son." He held out the blanket bundle and Tucker dropped Zoe's hand as the doctor placed the child in Tucker's arms, then turned to Unicorn Lady to answer her last question. "He'd be a ten but since he's two weeks early, mark him a nine on the Apgar just to be safe. We'll want to watch for jaundice so get a bilirubin count on him."

Tucker didn't breathe as he stared down at the crinkled face of the little boy. The child yawned, jamming a tiny fist in his mouth. A firm hand landed on his shoulder.

"Remember to breathe, Dad."

Yeah, about that. He really needed to explain the situation since Zoe hadn't. Tucker hadn't taken his eyes off the baby, and now realized he'd settled onto the edge of the bed close to Zoe and that her hand rested on his arm next to the baby's head. The words refused to come.

The pediatrician reached for the baby and Tucker discovered he was reluctant to let go. "Now that you've had some daddy bonding time, this little guy needs to try to eat. You had planned on breastfeeding, right, Zoe?"

Another nurse bustled in. "Her room is ready. We'll move her once she's fed the baby."

Tucker was still wrapping his head around the idea of breastfeeding as the doctor took the baby. Unicorn Lady moved in to help Zoe get situated. Before he could gather his wits, he and Zoe were alone in the cubicle and the little one was making happy noises beneath the blanket that covered Zoe's breasts. Slightly embarrassed by this most private event, Tucker turned to leave.

"No!" Zoe rasped out. Her panic was back. "I can't go to a room. I can't stay here." She lowered her eyes, as if ashamed. "I ain't got the money to stay in the hospital. Heck, I can't pay for the ambulance or this ER." She bit her bottom lip as it trembled.

Instinct had him cupping her cheek. There was no way he could walk away and leave her in this mess. She continued talking. "I had money saved for a birthing center and midwife and had one picked out here in

Nashville, but Bugtussle here blew that plan. I didn't exactly have time to get settled and make appointments." She glanced down before meeting his gaze again. "I don't like owin' people, have always paid my own way." A tear escaped and rolled down her cheek. "I don't know what to do."

"I do." He brushed a stray hair from her forehead. "I'll guarantee your bill." She opened her mouth to protest but he stopped her with a gentle finger laid over her lips. "Shh. I got this. We'll work out a way for you to pay it off."

She pressed back against the pillow so she could look into his eyes. An expression of resignation tinged with relief suffused her face. "I *will* pay you back."

"Damn straight you will." He said the words with a hint of humor in his voice.

Unicorn Lady returned with the other nurse and two orderlies. "I know you want to stay with the family, Dad, but time to deal with business." She ushered him from the room while the medical personnel bustled Zoe and her baby deeper into the hospital. By the time Tucker had explained the situation and dealt with payment details in the business office, his phone had blown up with messages. The whole gang from Bent Star had gathered in the ER waiting room. He strolled in to find balloons, flowers, teddy bears and bubble gum cigars—both pink and blue.

"It's a boy," he announced. "Seven pounds, ten ounces, and twenty inches long. Baby and mother are both doing fine. They want to keep her at least overnight to make sure things are all working correctly."

The entire group trooped to the maternity wing, leaving all the pink items at the nurses station to be passed out to the families with baby girls in the nursery. Having Deacon and the Sons of Nashville on the floor flustered the staff and caused curious faces to peek out through the doorways of patients' rooms. Since visitors were limited, the guys happily schmoozed with medical personnel and new moms alike.

Zoe, with her sleeping baby in a bassinet, was napping, but one by one, under Tucker's watchful gaze, the band members tiptoed in to admire the little boy and leave their gifts so she'd wake up to a plethora of flowers and balloons. Deacon leaned against the wall outside her room while Tucker shuffled from foot to foot under his brother's scrutiny.

"What?" Tucker knew he sounded defensive but didn't care.

"You wanna tell me what's the deal with this girl?"

"There is no *deal*."

"Uh-huh."

"Seriously, Deke." Tucker lifted his hand, wanting to rub his temple, then stopped himself. "Look, I found her on the side of the road." *Wearing a wedding dress and kicking the door of a classic Trans Am.* "She was having car trouble and needed a ride to Nashville. That's it. End of story."

"Uh-huh." Deacon's lips twitched. "Don't make me call Mom."

Dropping his head, Tucker gave in to the need to rub his forehead. "She was wearing a wedding dress. I had no idea she was pregnant."

"Whoa. Back up. Wedding dress? This sounds like a story where I need a beer in my hand while I'm listening."

"It's a long one, Deacon. The kid is basically alone and I felt sorry for her, so instead of dumping her at the first truck stop, I brought her to Nashville."

"So what now?"

"I don't know. She texted a friend but he's out of town. She has no place to stay. I do know she doesn't have much money, and no support system. What was I supposed to do?" He pinched the bridge of his nose. "I offered to buy her dinner and to help her figure things out. I…brought her inside. And now this."

"Maybe I *should* call Mom."

Tucker panicked and clenched his fingers in his brother's shirt. "No! Just…no."

"So what are you going to do?"

Releasing Deke with an embarrassed shrug, he stepped back and glanced inside Zoe's room. "There's room at the town house."

"You should call Bridger. He and Cash can check her out."

"Yeah. I should." He curled his lips between his teeth and gave a series of short nods. "I feel sorry for her, Deke."

His brother inspected him for what seemed like a very long time. "What else do you feel for her, Tuck?"

That was the rub, wasn't it? What *did* he feel beyond a hint of pity wrapped up with admiration? There was a tug of sexual attraction—okay, it felt more like a sledgehammer to the back of his head—but that feeling was seasoned with a lot of respect for her as a person. And watching her panic had brought out every protective bone in his body.

He glanced at Deacon. "She doesn't have much, is almost too proud to ask for help. I feel like doing that. Helping her out. So, that's what I'm doing."

"If Quin was here, I'd have her go shopping with you," Deke finally said. "You need to call the Bee Dubyas and get a list of what Zoe needs for the baby."

Calling any of the women married to his Barron cousins ranked right up there with calling his mother. "Why can't I call Quin?"

Deke laughed and three nurses stopped midstride to moon over him. "Because my beautiful wife is as new to motherhood as I am to being a father. The Bees have it down to a science."

Collectively, the Barron Wives were a force of nature. Still, better them than Katherine Tate. His mother would be on the next plane to Nashville. Deke patted him on the shoulder and said the words that meant Tuck owed him big time.

"I'll call Jolie and ask her to make a list of the fundamentals and email it to you."

When Zoe woke up the next morning, she found a fancy diaper bag and clothes—for her and Bugtussle. She hadn't decided on a name yet and she wasn't about to use his birth father's name. The room was full of flowers and balloons and she got misty-eyed. Was this what it felt like to have a family? To have friends? She'd been on her own for a very long time and hadn't stopped in any one place to put down those kinds of roots. Tucker had to be behind this, or maybe the band, because she'd lay odds the hospital didn't have a new baby welcoming committee with this kind of swag.

A female doctor breezed in, followed by a nurse. "Good morning, Zoe. I'm Dr. Sagawa. We met briefly last evening."

Zoe's smile was tentative, but she admired the woman's no-nonsense manner. "I need to take a look to make sure everything is still fine." The nurse took Zoe's vital signs while Dr. Sagawa gave her a checkup. "You're in remarkable shape. I'd release you today but Dr. Lucci wants to keep your baby at least another twenty-four hours. He has some concerns about jaundice."

"Is he okay?" Zoe leaned forward, her elbows braced against the partially raised bed.

Dr. Sagawa shrugged. "Not my department. Dr. Lucci will be in when he finishes rounds." The woman looked up and blinked. Zoe felt like all the blood had drained from her face. "No, no, Zoe. I'm sorry. My bedside manner is…well, technically, the baby isn't my responsibility, but everything is fine. Dr. Lucci always errs on the side of caution." She patted Zoe's shoulder. "An abundance of it," she mumbled, then added in a normal voice, "Since the little guy came early, we just want to make sure he's healthy before we release you."

After a few more minutes, the doctor bustled out, leaving the nurse to fuss over Zoe. Five minutes later, a second nurse arrived, cradling a swaddled baby in her arms. She scanned Zoe's armband, then the baby's to make sure the microchips matched, then she helped get everyone settled for feeding.

After the semi-successful feeding, with Bugtussle napping in her arms, Zoe considered her options. She closed her eyes and scrubbed at her forehead with the heel of one hand. She needed to find a job. And a place to live. And a babysitter so she could work that job—all things she'd planned to do once she escaped and got to Nashville. Tears leaked from her eyes. She brushed them away with an angry swipe. She'd been in tight corners before. She'd fight her way out of this one.

Zoe looked down at the sleeping baby and felt the smile tugging at her lips, despite her tears. Her baby. He was perfect. And she loved him more than life.

Movement and the soft clearing of a throat jerked her attention to the doorway. Despite his care and concern, she hadn't truly expected to see Tucker or anyone else. In her experience, rich folks like them didn't get involved with people like her. Finding Deacon Tate standing there left her speechless. And embarrassed.

"May I come in?"

She nodded mutely.

He stepped closer and leaned forward to see the baby. "Good-lookin' boy," he said with a big smile.

Zoe nodded again, feeling like a bobblehead doll.

Deacon chuckled. He hooked the leg of the visitor chair with a booted foot and pulled it closer to the bed. He sat and offered her another dazzling smile. "Tucker would have been here, but he was called back to Las Vegas on an emergency."

Eyes wide, she swallowed. "Las Vegas?"

"My little brother is mostly based out of Vegas. He's in charge of the Crown Casino and Resort. Heck, Tuck has his fingers in every Barron Entertainment business. Our cousin, Chase Barron, depends on him to keep things running smoothly. But if not for whatever went down in Vegas, I'm pretty sure he'd have been camped out here all night."

Zoe jerked back against the raised bed, blinking rapidly in surprise. "Why would he do that?"

Deke laughed. "He's a Tate, Zoe. It's the way we're wired."

How should she respond to that? While she hadn't expected the Tates to stick around, she'd really hoped Tucker would. She'd pretended not to be disappointed and learning that he would have been there created all sorts of warm feelings in her chest—feelings she shouldn't feel. She hated to admit, especially to herself, that she felt safe when Tucker was there. She opened her mouth but only one word came out, breathy at that. "Okay…"

"In the meantime, we need to talk."

"We do?"

"Yes. Do you have any place to go?" Zoe lowered her eyes, unable to meet Deke's. He followed up with a second question. "Job?"

"No," she mumbled. Then her pride asserted itself. She raised her head and met his gaze dead-on. "I'll figure it out. I always do. I'm not afraid of hard work and I always pay my own way."

His smile was approving as Deke continued, "From the discussion I had with Tuck, I sorta figured that's what you'd say. Two things. First, the company has a condo. You can stay there until you get your feet on the ground." She sucked in air to protest but he cut her off with one of his devastating smiles. "No argument. The place is sitting empty as long as Tucker's in Vegas. You might as well use it. Okay?" He waited until she nodded.

"Good. Now second, there's someone I'd like you to meet." She scowled and he held up his hands, palms out, to delay her response. "He's an old friend of mine. In fact, he helped me get my first gig here in Nashville. I played your video for him."

"My video?" She was completely confused. "What video?"

"The one Kenji recorded on his cell phone yesterday. Of you and me singing." He rolled his eyes. "He might be the best drummer in Nashville but that dude is far too attached to his smartphone apps."

Heat suffused her face and she just managed to resist fanning her cheeks. "Oh?" The word came out strangled.

"Don wants to meet you. He's mostly retired these days, but there's not an agent around who understands the music business better than him." Deke paused, watching. Zoe held her breath. "I can set that up after you're released, assuming you want to be in the music business?"

She remembered to breathe and played the bobblehead again. "Oh, yes!" she exclaimed. "That's the whole reason I came to Nashville."

Five

Tucker rubbed the back of his neck in a vain attempt to ease the low-level headache throbbing behind his eyes. He'd caught a late flight from Nashville to Las Vegas, and though he'd been in first class, he remembered why he preferred the company jet to flying commercial. He walked into his office at 8:00 a.m. freshly showered but with no sleep.

Janet, the administrative assistant who served both him and Chase, rose as he entered. She paused long enough to pour him a cup of coffee, grab the bottle of acetaminophen, then followed him into his office.

"Ever the model of efficiency, Jan." He offered her a sour smile as she handed him two capsules and the coffee mug. He tossed the pills into his mouth and took a big swig.

"You're welcome, boss. Bart is on his way up."

He resisted the urge to grumble. If the security chief for the casino was up and moving this early, that meant he'd gotten even less sleep than Tucker. He'd at least been able to catch an hour's nap on the flight. Tucker tapped his finger on the back of his cell phone, debating whether to call the hospital to check on Zoe and the baby. Ridiculous thought. Why would he want to check up on them? They weren't his responsibility. Not exactly.

Except he felt like they were. He needed to find out if the baby had developed jaundice, if Zoe had slept well. Deke promised to look after them while he was out of town, though his brother had ulterior motives.

Zoe had talent. He'd heard it, had seen Deke and the band react to that impromptu concert at Bent Star. And Deke hadn't freaked out that Zoe was playing his prized Gibson guitar. That said a lot right there. He should call Deke, talk to him about Zoe. Her talent, he amended, when he realized his slacks weren't so slack anymore. Good grief. The woman had just given birth and here he was—

"Sorry to make you fly in like this, Tucker."

Tuck glared up at the man standing in front of his desk. Bart Stevens wore a hand-tailored suit that looked like it had come off the discount rack. He was as big as a football linebacker and one look made a person think cop, soldier or mafia hitman. He'd been the first two and Tucker wasn't entirely certain about the third. Bart accepted a mug from Jan then waited for her to settle in one of the guest chairs before he took the other.

"So," Tucker began. "What's the problem?"

Three hours later, he wanted to rip out his hair but it was too short. The headache had bloomed into a full-blown migraine and there weren't enough pain pills in Las Vegas to touch it. The debrief by his staff didn't take long at all. To quote one of his mother's favorite expressions, things had gone to hell in a handbasket. There were two fires to put out. The first crisis would take some hands-on negotiation. The service workers union was making threats of a work slowdown. Tucker put that one on the back burner. The second involved a major whale.

Whale was a term he wasn't overly fond of, but was the way all the casinos referred to the people who dropped big bucks on the tables. The casinos sweetened the pot with perks like free rooms, drinks and other fringe benefits but sometimes there were problems. In this instance, it seemed one of the cocktail waitresses didn't appreciate a particular whale's wandering hands. Rather than create a scene, she reported the man to the bartender who notified the manager, who then assigned a male waiter. The whale took offense. Security was called. When Tucker approached him, the whale threatened to sue. Tucker suggested he'd get bigger perks at another hotel. The jerk was still muttering insults and invectives as staff settled him into the back of the hotel's limousine and sent him down the street. Tucker turned to his security chief and banned the whale. Nobody harassed his staff like that.

Now it was back to the first crisis. The threatened walkout would take time. Which meant he'd have to stay longer in Vegas. He should have been happy about returning to his normal routine, but every time he closed his eyes, he saw a pair of warm brown eyes, a pert nose and a mouth he really wanted to kiss. It didn't help that when he rode up to his suite, he shared the elevator with a couple and their baby. He caught himself before asking if he could hold the kid. What in the world was wrong with him?

Tucker entered his suite on the penthouse floor. He glanced at his expensive wristwatch and did some quick math. Then he pulled his cell phone out and called Nashville.

Deke ducked out into the hall while a nurse helped Zoe clean up. She heard his phone ring and wondered if maybe it was Tucker. She really needed to stop thinking about him. "Your guydar is broken bad," she muttered to herself.

With some wincing and ouching, Zoe made it to the small bathroom. The nurse untied the strings on the hospital gown and helped her sit on a plastic stool. "I have some shampoo in my duffel bag," Zoe said.

"I'll get it and I'll grab one of the pretty gowns that arrived."

Twenty minutes later, Zoe was clean, and her hair—still wet—was tamed and braided. She had a touch of makeup on and wore a short shell pink nursing nightgown with a matching pink-and-white striped robe. The nurse helped her settle in bed, then opened the door. Deacon waited in the hall, looking amused. As the nurse slipped out, he walked to the bed, cell phone in hand. He punched in numbers, then handed her the phone and walked out.

"Zoe?"

She blinked at the male voice and her heart hammered for a panicked moment. Then she recognized it. Not Redmond. Not Norbert. Tucker. She exhaled in relief. "Howdy, cowboy."

"Are you okay?"

"I'm fine."

"That's…ah…good." He sounded odd, like he didn't quite know what to say and she wondered if he felt as awkward as she did. Then he added, "So…have you talked to Deke?"

"Deke?"

"Yes. About staying at the condo. I'm stuck here in Vegas for a while."

Zoe didn't understand why his staying away longer would make her sad but it did. She didn't realize until that moment that she'd been counting on seeing him. Soon. "Oh."

As if he'd picked up on how small she was feeling, Tucker's voice dropped lower and he said very gently, "I'll be back as soon as I can. Until then, please, will you stay at the condo? Deke and his wife are just next door, and he's offered his nanny's expertise."

The idea of being alone in some strange condo worried her but his last statement gave her the reassurance she needed. There'd be someone nearby to help. All she had to do was say yes. Her pride reared its head, but she smacked it across the nose with a rolled-up newspaper. She had Baby Bugtussle to think about now. She sucked in a deep breath, exhaled to ease her anxiety and said, “Okay.”

“Okay?” Tucker sounded surprised…and relieved.

“Yeah, cowboy. Okay.”

Zoe awoke the next morning to a nurse checking her vitals. “Is it time to feed Bugtussle again?” she mumbled.

The nurse chuckled as she stuck the thermometer in Zoe’s mouth. “Good morning. And no, not quite yet. Looks like you and the baby will get to go home today.”

She blinked the grit out of her eyes and noticed the weak sunlight streaming in through the window. Real morning. Not for the first time, she wished for coffee. Yeah, no love there. Not until the baby was on a bottle and food. Dang it. Zoe rubbed her face and hoped breakfast would arrive before she was discharged. This whole eating-for-two thing was playing havoc with her appetite.

A firm tap on the door interrupted her thoughts. “Yeah?” she called.

The door eased open and a pretty African American girl peeked in. “Zoe?”

“That would be me.”

“Hi! I’m Keisha Selmon. I work for Deacon and Quin Tate as their nanny. Deke asked me to come by and help out.” She nudged the door with her shoulder and stepped in. She had bags and bundles and a fancy baby carrier. “Once you and the little one are discharged, I’ll take you to the condo and help you get settled in. In the meantime, I'll show you how all this paraphernalia works."

Zoe snapped her mouth shut and heard the nurse *tsk*. "Your blood pressure just spiked, young lady," the woman scolded. "Just calm down. This is all good."

Nodding, Zoe tried to tally up how much she would owe everyone. As if Keisha could read her mind, she forged ahead.

"This is all good, Zoe. You need to just relax. Let some nice people do nice things for you. Trust me. Deacon and Quin do stuff like this all the time. And don't even get me started on the Bee Dubyas."

"The what?"

Keisha laughed and fluttered her hand as if waving away any explanation. "You really don't want to know. Suffice it to say that I work for some very nice people who can and will help others. You're in a tight spot so they're helping." She deposited everything on the chair but one bag. "Quin and I guessed on sizes. If the jeans are too big, there's a belt. I hope you have shoes. We didn't want to take a chance guessing the size on those."

An hour later, after the doctors checked Zoe over and gave the baby a clean bill of health, a nurse came in to help her dress. Surprisingly, everything fit, and the baby looked darling in a onesie decorated with embroidered cowboy boots and guitars. She could only guess who chose that outfit.

She settled into the wheelchair the nurse insisted she ride in, then smiled as Keisha handed the baby to her.

"The guys are waiting to box all this stuff up, Zoe,

and they'll take it to the condo for you," Keisha said, gesturing at the flowers, balloons and stuffed animals that filled the room. "I suggest that you pick out maybe a couple of plants and a flower arrangement or two, then let the nurses spread the rest around?"

Zoe gave a distracted nod, then said, "Uh…the guys?"

"The guys in the band. They've been talking nonstop about you and the baby. When Tucker called Deacon for volunteers, they fell all over themselves wanting to help." Keisha glanced around as if someone might be eavesdropping before leaning closer. "Tucker is driving Deacon nuts. He can't get away from whatever is happening in Vegas and he calls all the time, wanting updates." She deepened her voice. "Is the condo ready? Did you babyproof it? Is there food?" She straightened and rolled her eyes. "That man, I swear."

When Zoe had finished with the discharge paperwork, a nurse wheeled her and the baby out of the hospital. Keisha waited beside a silver SUV idling under the covered portico at the medical center's door. The base for the carrier was already installed in the back seat. Keisha showed her how it all worked and once the baby was in place, the nanny helped Zoe into the SUV beside the baby. Dillon Tate turned around from the driver's seat.

"You ready, sugar?"

For the first time in ages, Zoe didn't feel weighed down by the world. She flashed a grin at Tucker's youngest brother. "Ready and willin'."

Zoe flicked her attention between the baby and the

scenery passing outside the window. The university campus gave way to a mixed-use area of shops, restaurants and residential. The SUV stopped at a stop sign and Dillon hit the left-turn signal. She leaned over the baby seat to stare out the passenger side window at a park with a large, Greek-inspired building in the center. “Is that the Parthenon?” She’d read about it—and everything else about Nashville she could get her hands on.

“That would be it,” Dillon agreed. He turned left onto Parthenon Avenue and drove a block. “Here we are. I’ll go around the block so you can see the place from the front.”

She sucked in a breath a few moments later as he pointed to a group of town houses. The corner unit was a huge, white granite edifice that echoed the Parthenon’s Greek influences. There was a smaller, brick unit that looked sort of English on the right.

“The brick condo is where you’ll be staying. Believe it or not, the Greek thing on the corner belongs to Deacon.” He circled the block then turned down a paved alley. Stopping at an iron gate, he hit a clicker button on the visor and the gate swung open so he could drive through.

After parking in the private garage, Dillon helped her out and then showed her how to release the carrier. He winked and admitted, “I practiced all last night to make sure I could do it right and not jostle Junior here.”

She stiffened as her heart did a funny lurch in her chest. Her baby would never be a junior—especially not a junior Tate. That said, he still needed a name. She was mulling over names as Dillon, still holding the carrier, ushered her and Keisha into an elevator. Who had elevators in their houses?

When the doors opened, they stepped out into a hallway. Dillon pointed toward the front of the house. "That's the master suite." Zoe held her breath then released it with a relieved huff when he pointed in the opposite direction. "That's the largest guest room. It has a private bath. C'mon."

He led the way and when he opened the door, all she could do was stand there and stare. If this was a guest room, the master suite must be magnificent. The queen-size bed was covered in a downy coverlet the color of a favorite pair of denim jeans. The head- and footboards were the color of aged barnwood and the walls were polished stucco the color of parchment. Where there'd once most likely been a sitting area, someone had set up a crib, rocking chair and baby accoutrements.

Dillon put the carrier down on the bed and scrubbed at the back of his head. "I have no clue what 90 percent of this stuff is. I hope the store left the instruction booklets."

Turning around in a slow circle, her arms outstretched, Zoe fought the tears burning in her eyes. "Who did all this?"

He flashed her a dimpled grin, looping an arm around Keisha's neck. "Tucker, of course. Well…sort of. He got the list from the Bee Dubyas, called the baby store, and told them to deliver and set everything up."

"Tucker did this?" She stared at Dillon and Keisha.

Dillon stared back. "Well…yeah."

Six

Resisting the urge to throw the computer against the far wall took far more effort than it should have. Tucker read the information scrolling across the monitor with a jaundiced eye. Someone was stirring up the union against several Barron properties. And someone else—or perhaps the same someone—had tried to block building permits necessary for two different Barron projects. He'd sent the info to Chase, along with Chance Barron, the family legal eagle, and to his brother Bridger and Cash Barron at Barron Security for further investigation.

Tucker grabbed the mug at his elbow and took a swig. Sputtering, it was all he could do not to spit cold coffee all over the keyboard. He caught the smirk Janet didn't hide in time. "I hate cold coffee," he groused.

Without a word, his very efficient assistant snagged the mug, emptied it in the sink on the coffee bar across the room, poured him a fresh cup and returned to set it carefully at his elbow before she settled one hip on the corner of his desk.

"Wanna tell me why you're in such a foul mood, boss man?"

"No." Okay, he sounded as pouty as a teenager. He wasn't sulking. Much. He didn't want to be here in Vegas. He wanted to be in Nashville. He glanced up to find Janet staring down at him.

"Gotta be a woman."

He pushed away from the desk, leaned back in his chair and challenged her with a quirked brow. "And how did you come to that conclusion?"

"C'mon, boss. You know this place is a rumor mill. Besides, ENC already has an online spread with pictures of you at the hospital in Nashville."

Tucker dropped his head and closed his eyes. The Entertainment News Channel could be a real pain in his ass—unless he was the one manipulating the stories. He'd have to get Barron Entertainment's PR department to start damage control. Pinching the bridge of his nose, he glanced up. "How bad is it?"

Janet shrugged. "Pictures don't show much. A woman on a gurney holding something in her arms all bundled up. You climbing out of the ambulance looking shell-shocked. Pictures taken in the waiting room of Deacon and the band with flowers and balloons—pink *and* blue. Which was it, by the way?"

"Boy."

"You want to explain who the girl is?"

He started to say "nobody," but that wasn't true. Zoe Parker was somebody. And so was her baby. His chest tightened as he remembered looking down into the baby's eyes that first time. Tucker wasn't one to willingly explore feelings. They were fine for everyone else and he was more than happy to offer advice to his brothers and cousins. But when it came to him personally? Nope. "She's a singer Deacon was auditioning, and she went into premature labor."

"Uh-huh." Janet wore a dubious look that said loud and clear she didn't believe him for a minute. "So why were you in the ambulance with her?"

Why had he been in the ambulance with her? Oh yeah, because he'd been hovering and the EMT mistook him for the father. Yeah, that bit shouldn't get out. Because he wasn't the father. And he didn't have feelings for Zoe. Or her baby. Except…maybe he did.

"I…she didn't want to ride alone. No one expected the baby to come as fast as he did."

Laughing, Janet stood up. "I can see it now. You sittin' there wringing your hands, saying over and over you know nothing about birthing babies."

He would have laughed along except he'd pretty much been thinking that at the time. "Shut up, Janet. Don't you have real work to do or something?"

"Or something." She sashayed to the office door where she paused and glanced back over her shoulder in a dramatic gesture. In a purely fake Southern accent, Janet announced, "After all, tomorrow is another day."

"Shut the door behind you," Tucker growled. Tomorrow *was* another day—another day he didn't want to be here. He needed to be back in Nashville and that was messed up beyond belief.

He swiveled his desk chair so he could gaze out the window. The view wasn't all that great as they were only on the fourth floor, but it beat staring at the walls of his office. What was it about Zoe Parker that drew him like a hungry man to a T-bone steak? She wasn't beautiful. She was cute and quirky. She had Dolly Parton's sense of style. Which was cute and quirky. She was a single mother—a cute and quirky single mother, and when her son had stared up at him with those big, luminous blue eyes, Tucker had fallen hard. He totally understood Deacon now. When a baby had been left on Deke's tour bus with a note claiming he was the father, his big brother had fallen for the angelic baby named Noelle, even though he wasn't her father. Deke married Quin, the Oklahoma Highway Patrol officer assigned to the case, and they'd adopted her.

Business. Tucker needed to keep his thoughts on business. He couldn't get back to Nashville until he cleared his desk here in Vegas. Damn. He was in so much trouble.

Tucker swiveled back to his desk and snatched the phone receiver. With the first call, he requested that the company plane be ready to fly him to Nashville at a moment's notice. The second call went straight to his brother Bridger.

"What's up, Tuck?"

"Did you get my email about the stuff going on with the union and those permits?"

"Sure did. Cash has called a meeting. Can we patch you in via the closed-circuit link?"

"Set it up with Janet. In the meantime, I have something else I want you to check out, little bro."

Zoe didn't breathe for a minute. Asleep. She'd been asleep. Something woke her. Where was she? Heart beating as fast as a hummingbird's, she forced air into her lungs. She sat up and peered through the twilight filling the room. She heard a small hiccupping cry and her breasts were suddenly swollen. The baby was awake, and hungry. They were in Nashville. In the guest room at Tucker's condo. Safe.

Shadows lurked in the corners of the room though streetlights sparkled outside. She caught the faint hum of traffic but no other sounds. Rolling off the bed, she reached into the crib and gathered her baby into her arms. Zoe nuzzled the dark fuzz on his head as she settled onto the comfortable rocking chair and got him situated so he could nurse. She hummed softly as she watched the city lights through the window.

A sense of peace settled around her and her nonsensical hum began to form a melody. She drifted along, everything right in her world. Then the door creaked open and part of a face peered at her. Zoe let out a scream and scrambled to her feet, looking for a weapon.

"Whoa!" a familiar voice said. "Easy, there. It's just me, Zoe."

She collapsed into the rocker, her mouth dry and her heart galloping. "Don't scare a body like that, Tucker!"

"I'm sorry. It's late. I thought you'd be asleep. I just wanted to check on you."

She inhaled, glad the room was dark as she got herself put back together. Still hungry, the baby nuzzled in. She cuddled him, all the while watching the very handsome man standing in the doorway.

"Didn't expect you back." She hadn't but now that he was? Her heart was still beating fast but for an entirely different reason. "But I gotta say I'm glad. Ramblin' around in this big ol' house alone is…" She lost her train of thought as he came into the room and stood staring down at her. She patted her hair, the gesture self-conscious. "I must look a fright."

"No," he said, his voice husky. "You look…" He swallowed and smiled. "You look just fine, Zoe."

They stared at each other for a long moment then he cleared his throat. "I guess I should let you two get back to sleep."

"Yeah, it is sorta late an' all."

Tucker backtracked toward the door but then paused. "Are you hungry?" he blurted out, then hastily added "I picked up some stuff for sandwiches on my way in from the airport. Or I can order takeout. You know, if sandwiches don't appeal."

Her stomach grumbled, and she giggled. "I suppose I might be. A sandwich sounds just fine."

"Do you need any help?" He stepped closer.

Zoe patted the baby's bottom and smiled. "He'll be full in a minute. If you can grab that carryall thing, I'll just get Bugtussle settled when he's done and then we can head down to the kitchen."

Tucker didn't move. He just stood there and stared, as if transfixed by the scene.

"Tucker?"

He startled when she said his name. "Yeah. Carrier. I'm on that."

A few minutes later, Zoe sat on a leather and wrought-iron stool watching Tucker preparing sandwiches on the other side of the high bar separating the dining area from the kitchen. The baby cooed in the carrier and gurgled at her when she reached over to tickle his toes. She gave Tucker directions on building her sandwich.

He paused, squeeze bottle of mustard in his hand, and stared at her. "How are you really? Has Keisha been helping?" He squeezed out some mustard. "I know she's busy with Noelle and all. Maybe I should hire a nurse to come in for a few days."

Zoe studied him. He sounded so…something. He was at once insistent and insecure, an odd combination for this man who had the world at his fingertips. She couldn't resist saying, "Okay."

He continued talking, like he hadn't heard her. "You won't owe me anything. Despite rumors to the contrary, I can be a nice guy. Having a new baby is hard, even when there's not much to clean or look after. And… well…it seems I've sort of adopted you and—" He glanced over to the baby and frowned. "Have you decided on a name yet?" The abrupt change in subject came with a silly googly-eyed face he made at her baby. "Bugtussle Parker is just plain mean."

Zoe burst out laughing, startling both the baby and

the man. "Oh, I don't know. I think it has a certain ring to it. Your brother Dillon calls him Junior." She reached over and grabbed the baby's feet, kissing them which made him coo again.

When she glanced up, the expression on Tucker's face rocked her down to her very toes. He looked like he'd been mule kicked. His gaze was full of longing, like he hungered for something he couldn't have. Had her comment about Dillon caused this response? She remembered her own reaction the first time Dillon called her son that. No, Bugtussle would never be a junior, but someday, if the two of them were lucky, he'd be the son of a good man—a man like the one fixing her a sandwich in the middle of the night because he was lonely but wouldn't admit it.

He watched the baby now and there was an inherent sweetness in his look that revealed a side to Tucker Tate she'd never expected to see. Her heart melted more than a little, despite the stern lecture she was mentally giving it. Hooking up with Tucker was wrong on so many levels. They came from different worlds. He lived in luxury and everything she owned fit in an old army duffle and her guitar case. He was a nice guy and she was the single mother of another man's baby.

Was it possible that being wrong just might be right this time? She sneaked a look at him and told herself not to hope.

Seven

Zoe did her very best not to fidget. She'd been staying at Tucker's for over a week. He'd been sweet and supportive, and she figured they were on their way to being friends if not something—nope. She was not gonna go there. She was already nervous enough.

Tucker had left for work when Deacon called to tell her about this meeting. She'd left Bugtussle with Keisha and Noelle and gotten ready.

Deacon had given her the thumbs-up when he picked her up to bring her to the Bent Star offices. She wore faded jeans, a really cool top in a Native American print that slipped off one shoulder and her lucky Ariat boots. She had her guitar, though Deacon had offered her his very sweet Gibson. She was ready. Maybe.

A knock on the door convinced her she wasn't. She

sucked in a deep breath when Deacon smiled at her. "You got this, darlin'." Louder, he called, "C'mon in."

Deacon approached the other man and they shook hands. "Thanks for coming, Don. I'd like to introduce you to Miss Zoe Parker."

The agent looked to be in his seventies, with a shock of silver hair and a trimmed mustache. He walked over to Zoe and offered his hand. "Don Easley," he said.

Laughing, Deke added, "Most people know him as Dandy Don Easley."

Zoe's heart skipped a beat. *That* name she recognized. Dandy Don had guided some of the biggest names in country music for almost fifty years.

"I'm very pleased to meet you, Mr. Easley."

"Deke here tells me you can sing a little."

Her gaze darted between them, but she managed a slight tuck of her chin in the affirmative and a mumbled, "A little."

"Since we're in a recording studio, I'd like to hear you in person, as well as maybe lay down a track or two?" He glanced at Deacon and received a nod. "Wanna sing something for me?"

Voice frozen in her throat, Zoe figured her eyes must be the size of half-dollars. Deacon urged her to the stool sitting in front of a microphone and handed her the Martin D35 acoustic guitar she'd scrimped and saved for ages to buy. It was old and battered but still played sweet. She sat, settled the guitar in her lap and riffed a few chords.

"What would you like me to sing?" she asked without looking up.

"Let's do something vintage," Mr. Easley said. "Give me a little Dolly?"

Her fingers automatically found the chords for "Jolene." Her voice didn't have the distinct tonal qualities of Dolly's, but she could do a fair job with the song. She sang the first verse and chorus and when no one stopped her, she transitioned to Reba McEntire's "Fancy." After a couple of verses, Zoe's grin turned wicked as she plucked the opening to Miranda Lambert's "Gunpowder and Lead."

By the time she finished, the sound studio's control room was clogged with people, all listening. The last chord still hung in the air when the applause started. She searched the faces lining the window but didn't find the one she was looking for. She pretended not to be disappointed that Tucker wasn't there.

Zoe was pretty sure her blush ran all the way to the roots of her hair, but she didn't care. Her cheeks hurt from the big smile she wore and the approval on both the face of the country music star and the old man who'd started a whole bunch of careers had her blinking away unshed tears of happiness.

"Dang, darlin'." Mr. Easley sighed happily. "You an' me are gonna do some good things."

Over the course of the next hour, she explained her situation, including the fact she owed Tucker a bunch of money. Don eyed Deke, who hastened to explain. "My brother guaranteed her medical bill."

"And why would he do that?"

Deke grinned and Zoe wondered at the twinkle in

his eye. "Because the EMTs mistook him for the daddy and bein' a Tate, he stepped up."

Mr. Easley, who insisted she call him "Don," didn't blink an eye at that. After she explained her daddy had raised her to respect her elders, so it would have to be either Mr. Easley or Mr. Don, she went on to insist, "I gotta do this on my own talent, not because nice folks think I need a handout." Deke and the older man exchanged a look, but she kept on before they could interrupt. "I gotta pay my own way, Mr. Don. Period."

"Fine," Don agreed. "In the meantime, I have a guesthouse. The missus fixed it up when I started draggin' stray singers home. It's not fancy but it's clean. You can live in it until I make sure you earn enough to pay your way." He smiled and held out his hand. "You'll be makin' that soon enough, but it'll do for the time being. We gotta deal?"

She glanced over at Deacon, wondering if she should trust any of them. "Sugar, take this part on a handshake. When Dandy Don offers a real contract, I'll have my attorney look it over for you. Okay? Don's not offering representation yet so he's not taking a percentage."

"Not yet, but darlin', I think you've got a lot of talent. It won't be easy totin' a little one around and startin' from scratch. I'm mostly retired, but I like to keep my hand in the game from time to time. I can give you a safe place to live if you want to move out of Tucker's place. I can line up some gigs. None of it will rub any skin off my nose. You got talent. You show me the drive, and we'll probably do business. Deal?"

Zoe was pretty sure her face was going to break from the huge smile. She stuck out her hand.

"Deal."

Mr. Don didn't waste time. After her audition yesterday, he wanted Zoe in the studio first thing this morning. She didn't like elevators. But hauling the baby and all his paraphernalia up and down numerous flights of stairs in the condo was a struggle. Not to mention there was something far more interesting to leave her breathless besides climbing stairs.

And that something was standing there as the elevator door opened.

She sighed. Inwardly, of course. It wouldn't do—wouldn't do *at* all—for him to know how she felt.

Tucker Tate was just plain delicious. He could let his hair grow out but those blue eyes of his? And that little bit of scruff? She'd always been a sucker for a man who sported it. As he stood there towering over her, she felt petite. And pretty, because she was experienced enough to recognize appreciation for a woman in a man's eyes.

"Zoe." His voice was low, husky, and promised all sorts of things she wanted. Things she couldn't have. She squashed down the flicker of hope sparking in her chest. The only luck she had concerning men was bad.

She had to swallow before she said, "Tucker."

"Where you headed?"

"Bent Star. Deacon asked me to come down to the studio."

"I'll give you a ride."

Her mind went straight to a place it had no business being—and it wasn't the rodeo. She breathed out and licked her lips. His eyes lasered in on her mouth, then he leaned down. Oh, glory. Did he mean to kiss her? Her eyes drifted shut in anticipation.

"Got everything you need?" His lips almost touched hers as he spoke. All she had to do was purse hers and they'd be kissing. Then she felt the weight of the baby carrier lifted from her hand.

Zoe opened her eyes. Tucker was standing back, holding the carrier, and dang the man but he was grinning like he knew how hard her heart was pounding. She curled her lip in a little snarl. "I need to get my guitar. It's in the livin' room."

He slipped the diaper bag from her shoulder. "I'll put the kiddo in my car."

When they got to the Bent Star offices, Don Easley was waiting and without a backward glance hustled Zoe away. Tucker disappeared with the baby, still in his carrier. She was waved into the sound booth where Deacon and the band waited. Four grueling hours later, they broke for lunch. She was hoarse and gulped down the large glass of ice water the sound engineer handed her.

"Gotta say, sugar," he said with a grin. "You've got a distinctive voice."

She wasn't sure if that was a good thing or a bad thing. She was still considering the implications when Tucker arrived.

"Your boy's fussing. I changed him so I figure he's hungry and that's something I can't do."

Wait. What? Tucker *changed a dirty diaper?* She was speechless as he ushered her to his office. A woman about her age was walking the floor with the baby on her shoulder. Tucker's secretary, Zoe figured, and she looked so relieved Zoe had to smile.

About twenty minutes later, when she walked out of Tucker's private office with a full and happy baby, the man himself was waiting.

"I'll take you to lunch."

As they hit the front door, she added those to her list of famous last words. They stepped out into a yelling throng of paparazzi.

"Who's the girl, Tucker?"

"Tucker, is that your baby?"

"You gonna marry your baby momma, Tucker?"

The warm fuzzy moment of sizzle and almost kissing they'd shared that morning dissipated in the jumble of cameras. She'd been crazy. Crazy to dream about a singing career. And crazier to dream that something might be simmering between her and the handsome executive who was propelling her back inside the building.

Don Easley stood in the foyer, hands fisted on his hips. "Well, that settles it." He glared at Tucker as if that mob outside was all his fault. "They know where you live cuz Deacon lives right next door. Zoe's movin' into my guesthouse." Tucker opened his mouth like he planned to argue but Don cut him off. "No arguments, boy. Rosemary n'me, we'll take care of her and the little nipper."

"But—" Zoe began, only to be interrupted.

"No arguments. I've been handlin' the paparazzi longer than you—" Don stabbed a finger at Tucker "—or you have been alive."

Tucker's expression turned stubborn, but Don swept his arm out, encompassing the entrance. "You wanna live with all that commotion right outside your door? I know Deacon dang sure doesn't."

Zoe saw the moment Tucker capitulated. Maybe he was tired of having her and the baby underfoot. Maybe he wanted his life back.

"Fine." Tucker bit out the one word.

And that was that. Zoe's heart sank. Yeah, so much for pipe dreams. Especially that almost kiss.

Eight

Zoe pushed a heavy fall of hair over her shoulder as she nervously picked out a tune on the strings of her guitar. She sat in the dark hallway at the back of Calamity's waiting for her turn to sing. Mr. Don hadn't wasted any time in getting her this gig. Granted, it was only an open mic night, but he'd gotten her on the bill so she was guaranteed a spot. He appeared beside her, a big smile on his face.

"No reason to be nervous, sugar. Have you decided what to sing? You've got two numbers."

She tilted her head, thinking hard. "Is it better to do covers instead of my original stuff?"

Mr. Don rubbed his chin. "That's a good question, girl. I think for t'night, yeah. Do one up-tempo number to get 'em stirred up and then follow with a ballad. Got any ideas?"

Zoe let her fingers wander through some chords as she considered her options. The singer currently on the stage was doing his best to cover a Toby Keith song. That was chancy at best because Toby Keith was one of a kind. Whatever she did, she'd have to make sure her distinct talent shone through. She grinned. "I have a couple of ideas. I'll wait to decide once I'm out there and can gauge the audience."

The singer finished to lackluster applause, and he shuffled off the stage. Yup, she would have to bring out the big guns tonight. She wiped her sweaty palms on the short jean skirt she wore and stood up. The pregnancy hadn't affected her legs and the uppers on her favorite pair of boots climbed all the way to her knees. She'd opted for a loose top with some fringe on the bottom and a wide neck that dipped over her right shoulder when she strummed the guitar.

She moved to the edge of the stage, waiting while the announcer did his spiel. Mr. Don patted her shoulder. "Sing your heart out, girl. I'll be in the front row cheerin' you on." With that, he slipped away.

"Calamity's is pleased to welcome a newcomer to our fine stage tonight," the MC announced. There were some groans from the audience. On open mic night, that could mean a singer like the guy preceding her. She'd just have to prove them wrong. "Put your hands together for Zoe Parker."

A few people clapped enthusiastically, and she figured it came from Mr. Don's table. Plastering a big smile on her face, she strode onto the stage and slung her guitar behind her while she adjusted the microphone.

"Hey, y'all," she said, her voice husky. "I'm mighty pleased to be here tonight. We got any rednecks out there?" She lifted her hand to shade her eyes against the glare of the stage lights and surveyed the room. Zoe got a few whistles and yells as she pulled her guitar back into position to play. "We got any redneck women out there?" And before anyone could respond, she launched into Gretchen Wilson's rollicking "Redneck Woman."

By the end of the first stanza, she had the entire room eating out of her hand. When she got to the part in the second chorus asking for redneck girls in the audience to respond, they did with a big, "Hell, yeah!"

Zoe finished the song to screams, whistles, stomping feet and thunderous applause. She found Mr. Don in the audience, with his ear-to-ear grin, and choked as she recognized the other people at his table—Deacon Tate with a pretty woman tucked against his side, the rest of the Sons of Nashville, some with dates, some solo. And there, standing and whistling with his fingers between his lips was Tucker. Her heart lurched.

Her fingers plucked at the strings, almost of their own volition, and the crowd settled down. She knew the song she wanted to sing but Dierks Bentley's "Black" was a little too sexy for the situation because she did not need to be thinking those kinds of thoughts about Mr. Tucker Tate. Her left hand found the correct chords and she played the opening measure for Little Big Town's "Better Man" instead.

She did her best to let her gaze roam across the crowd, stopping and holding the eyes of an audience member as she would normally. Tonight wasn't normal. Tonight, her gaze kept lingering on Tucker. The song didn't fit him. The words spoke of love lost, of families divided, of emotional damage done in the name of that most elusive of emotions. But she couldn't help wondering just what kind of man he was. The words of the song spoke to her—mostly. She'd never been married, and she'd never truly been in love. Mainly because she had lousy luck and no sense of self-preservation when it came to the men she picked.

Tucker Tate was Armani suits and she was Daisy Dukes. He was aged bourbon and she was cheap beer. She almost missed a chord as her thoughts became the words to a song and matched with notes in her head. She needed to get off the stage so she could write the song down before it fluttered away. Pride, she reminded herself. She needed to show some and start living her life. She didn't need a man to take care of her. She never had. Never would. It didn't matter that Tucker was sitting there handsome as all get-out, those deep blue eyes of his watching her every move with a hungry look in them.

The hardest thing she'd ever done was pack up and move but Mr. Don was right. She couldn't live under the same roof with Tucker. Which was a dang shame. For that couple of weeks, she'd forgotten to be lonely.

That man was gonna be trouble and she needed to steer clear. She had a baby to raise—and she loved him with all her heart. Baby Bugtussle would always come first. But to take care of him, she needed a career, not just a job, and in between all that, she had a life to live. A life that didn't have room for a rich man with pretty blue eyes and a mouth that the devil himself would be jealous of. Tucker was a better kind of man, one that women would want to love. She couldn't afford to lose her heart.

Then he smiled at her.

Tucker had groused all the way downtown. He did *not* want to sit surrounded by the noise and crush of Calamity's. It was open mic night. He had things to do—like harassing the PR Department to work harder at quelling the rumors so the paparazzi would leave him and Zoe alone.

When he, Deacon and Quin arrived, the Sons of Nashville were already occupying a table just to the right of the stage. Pitchers of beer and mugs, baskets of pretzels and buckets of peanuts littered the crowded table. A couple of the guys had dates but they'd still managed to scrounge four extra chairs. Tuck eyed his brothers, wondering if they'd set him up with a blind date. Dillon was especially prone to doing so. Kenji filled three mugs with beer and passed them to the newcomers.

Quin's hands went to the neckline of her shirt. She fussed for a second then pulled out a Day-Glo orange hearing protector. She fitted the earplugs on the end of the band into her ears. Smart. He tapped her on the shoulder and pointed.

"Got any more of those?"

She laughed but shook her head. "You guys are on your own. I made the mistake of coming here when Deke decided to play one night. The noise level was insane."

Tucker rolled his eyes as he flashed her a thumbs-up. Deke was prone to do that. Toby Keith had a restaurant in Bricktown—the entertainment district near downtown Oklahoma City. Like Toby and other entertainers, Deke and the Sons had shown up there unannounced and played on more than one occasion. The locals and tourists alike lived for those moments. He wondered, since the whole band was here, if they had something planned for Calamity's.

The first act, a quartet, did decent covers of two Oak Ridge Boys songs. The second, a kid who looked to be about twelve, had trouble with his voice breaking. Ah, the joys of puberty. The third guy tried to imitate Keith and since there was and could be only one Toby, the natives were growing restless. As the announcer took the stage, Tucker looked up when Dandy Don Easley slid into the chair next to him. That could mean just one thing. Tucker sat up, his whole body vibrating.

He'd stayed away from Zoe for the two days since she'd moved into the Easleys' guesthouse, convincing himself that dropping by to check up on her and bring food would alert the paparazzi to her location. They'd been two of the longest days in his life. That first night, he lasted three hours. Then he camped out at Deacon and Quin's, playing with Noelle, and rummaging in their fridge for food. He wouldn't admit the empty condo bugged the hell out of him. Good thing

Deacon had bought the town house on the other side for the band. Last night, Quin had sent him next door to hang out with them.

Tucker wouldn't admit he missed Zoe and the baby, but here he was, leaning toward the stage impatient to see the woman he spent far too much time thinking about. The announcer introduced her and his chest got tight. The table erupted with applause and encouraging cheers, but Tuck knew the audience here at Calamity's. They hadn't been too thrilled with the last guy and now here was Zoe, a newcomer to the scene. *He* knew she could sing but these other loudmouths didn't. Would they settle down and give her a chance?

Zoe stepped to the microphone and Tucker forgot everything. When she launched into her first song, he felt it all the way down deep. The place went wild. She strummed that guitar and belted out the lyrics, owning the stage, the audience...and him. He was in so much trouble.

When she rolled over into "Better Man," he surrendered. He might as well carve out his heart and hand it to her on a silver platter because every time her eyes fell on him, she made him want to be the man she wanted, the man she needed. Which was just crazy. Love at first sight didn't happen. Despite what his mom said. She was convinced that each of her boys would meet the right woman and know immediately that she was the one. He glanced over at Quin and Deke. Their chairs sat side by side and his brother had one arm draped over her shoulders. They held hands and as he watched, they looked into each other's eyes, smiled and exchanged a soft kiss.

That was love. Real love. Deep love. The kind of love that a man found once in his life if he was the luckiest son of a gun around. His parents had that kind of love. And his cousins had found it. Deke had it. Tucker was all about business. Since Chase married Savannah, Tucker was all but running Barron Entertainment. He didn't have time for love. But being around Zoe and the baby? *Nope.* He stuffed those thoughts down deep, to be ignored. He would help her out but that was all.

He pulled his gaze away from the couple and focused once more on the stage. Surrounded by lights, Zoe all but glowed up there. Her hair fell in a long, soft wave and her bare shoulder peeked out from behind the silken curtain. He wanted to kiss that shoulder. And her neck. Her mouth. Her nose. He wanted to kiss her in far more intimate places, and he didn't give a flip that she was a new mother. Except he had to. She was vulnerable and too easy to take advantage of. Business. She needed to be business, not pleasure. Good thing he didn't have time to get involved with anyone, much less her.

She played the crowd like a pro, but her eyes returned to him time and again. His heart did weird things in his chest each time her gaze fell on him. The song was almost over, and she looked like she was living every word of the lyrics. He smiled at her. And something in her eyes gave him pause. Tucker needed to slam the brakes on. So what if he'd gotten used to having her—and her baby—around? Big deal. He traveled. A lot. He didn't want an anchor. He glanced around the table. Deacon and the band wanted him to sign her to Bent Star. She had a lot of talent. Another reason to stop his brain—and maybe his heart—from going places neither had any business being. He was a businessman. And he needed to keep things between them professional. So that's what he'd do. Period.

Then the song ended and the place erupted in cheers and whistles, hard applause and stomping boots. Everyone came to their feet. Zoe remained on the stage looking stunned. The announcer joined her, but the crowd didn't settle down, not even when he held up his hands for silence. They wanted more. For a fleeting second, Tucker felt sorry for the entertainer scheduled next. That's when he realized Deacon and the boys were on their feet and moving to the stage. He didn't think it possible for the noise level in the room to increase but it went up a hundred decibels.

Tuck chanced a quick glance at Quin. She sat, smug smile and ear protection firmly in place. She'd known. This wasn't some impromptu gig. Deke had planned it. Quin caught his eye and winked, then patted the chair beside her. He sank onto it, knowing now that the show was far from over. Zoe Parker was the new princess of the Nashville country music scene.

When the impromptu concert ended, Zoe, Deacon and the band disappeared backstage. Tucker ushered Quin, Don and the band's dates through the crowd. Quin and the girls rushed into the packed hallway to connect with their significant others. Tucker stood back, observing. Zoe, surrounded by people, positively glowing. She looked up and her gaze fell on him. Her face lit up like a Christmas tree and suddenly, she was flying toward him. She leaped. He caught her. And then their mouths clashed. Her legs circled his waist and he held her with one hand cupping her butt, the other the back of her head so he could control the kiss.

Time passed—seconds or minutes. Tucker wasn't sure. Then sound returned. Laughter. The buzz of conversation. Reality intruded, hitting him and Zoe at the same time. She unhooked her ankles. He loosened his grip. She slid to stand with both feet on the scuffed floor. Neither spoke and then she was gone, pulled into the group by Don, who was shouting over the hubbub. Tucker took a step back, astonished at what had just happened. That kiss had been…he didn't have the words. But watching Zoe walk away? He had a word for that. *No.*

Tucker stared at her retreating form. He wanted to hear her voice. He wanted to see her even more. Touch her. And that was just…no. Too many complications. He wanted to sign her to a record contract. He wanted to kiss her again. He wanted…

"I'd give a hundred bucks to know what you're thinking," Deacon said as he approached. "You know I can read you like a book, Tucker. You want to go after her."

"Oh yeah? If you're so sure of that, why did you offer me a hundred?"

"Conversation starter. Why don't you ask her out on an actual date?"

He considered the various answers he could offer

as justification—all the ones he'd been debating in his own head. "She's vulnerable."

Deke leaned his elbow against the wall beside Tucker's head and stared at him with an amused expression. "How so?"

"Seriously? You really have to ask?" Tucker held up a finger. "For one, she's all alone in Nashville. Two, she wants to be a singer. Three, she's a single mom. Four—"

"You like her and are attracted," Deacon interrupted. "There's nothing wrong with that. And…" He held up a finger. "She's not alone. Don Easley is looking out for her. Two, she *is* a singer, she just needs help with her career. Three, so what? I've seen you look at that baby, Tucker. The kid owns you." His grin was astute as he added, "I know that feeling well. I felt the same way about Noelle."

"Four," Tucker persisted, "she thinks she needs to pay me back and she's made it abundantly clear she wants to make it on her own. Five, business doesn't mix with pleasure. Refer back to number two."

"Mixing business and pleasure worked fine for cousin Clay. And Cash." Deke shrugged. "And technically, for me."

"It's complicated."

Deke burst out laughing. "Of course it is. We're Tates, little bro. If we didn't complicate things, we'd be…" He laughed again. "Well, not Barrons, because our cousins have *complicated* hardwired into their DNA."

"So you're blaming Mom for this?" Tucker tried hard to hide a smirk.

"Not goin' there. You saw how she was with Quin and Noelle. And you know there's a reason we call our irritating little brother Dill Pickle. He's probably called and told her everything. Do us all a favor? Just take her out. Get Zoe out of your system if it's only an attraction. If it's more, you'll know, and we'll all deal with it." Deacon straightened and patted his brother on the shoulder. "Just get a move on, Tuck. At the very least, I'd like her to open a few of our upcoming concerts. If you aren't going to date her, sign her. If you *are* going to date her, still sign her. She needs to understand that her talent and your horniness are not mutually exclusive."

Tucker heard his big brother laughing all the way down the hall as he rejoined the band and Zoe's fans who'd made their way backstage. He'd never been affected like this by a woman. Zoe slipped through all the cracks in the wall he threw up between them. Because she *was* business. She'd be a phenomenal addition to Bent Star's lineup of singers. He'd be a bad businessman if he didn't sign her. But he really, *really* wanted the pleasure of getting to know her better.

For the past three weeks, Zoe had pretended that she hadn't thrown her arms around Tucker Tate and kissed him in the aftermath of her successful debut at Calamity's. She'd pretended even harder that he hadn't kissed her back. Of course, the jerk hadn't called either—not that she was paying attention to whether he did or not, because she wasn't. Nope.

"We don't need a man in our lives, do we, Bugtussle?" The sleepy baby yawned and stared up at her with big eyes. She made big eyes back. "Our lives are full and you know it."

That was true. She had a gig at Calamity's playing a full set two nights a week and was hitting up other clubs for open mic nights. Money wasn't pouring in, but she was making enough to save up for a used car and put money in her Pay Tucker Back Fund. She'd splurged and bought a cell phone, and texted the number to Tucker...because. He'd texted back a quick Thanks. Her jumbled feelings for the dang man hadn't been helped when her doctor pronounced her healed at her six-week appointment.

"What's that mean, exactly?" she'd asked.

She blushed when Dr. Sagawa explained Zoe could "start dating" though not in those exact words. Zoe had insisted that she had absolutely no intention of getting involved with a man. Any man. Period. The doctor simply smiled in the way that doctors did, recognizing BS when she heard it. Of course, the only man who might get her stirred up was Tucker Tate, but he obviously wanted to keep things strictly business.

Despite that kiss. Hang the man. Why didn't he call?

Her cell phone chose that moment to dance across the tabletop, and she snatched it just as it tumbled over the edge. She had it on vibrate because the baby was sleeping. "Hello?" she answered, her voice a husky whisper.

"Zoe?"

"Yeah?"

"It's Tucker. You sound… Is everything okay?"

She knew who it was the moment he said her name. Her heart pounded with excitement. Stupid thing. He was just calling to check up on her. That's all. "The baby's asleep. Trying not to wake him."

"Oh." He sounded…hesitant?

Silence. She waited.

"Are you working tonight?"

Is that why he was calling? "No." Now she sounded hesitant.

"Would you like to go out?"

"Out?"

"Yes. Like…out. To dinner or something."

"Like a…date?" She held her breath.

"Yeah…sort of."

"What does that mean? A sorta date?" She glowered at the phone then realized she could hear Tucker breathing. Hard.

"I'm messing this up. I've been…thinking about you."

Uh-huh. Was he thinking about her like she'd been thinking about him? All tangled sheets, sweaty bodies and wet kisses? She reminded herself to breathe.

"I've been thinking things over. And, well…" He didn't finish his thought. She waited. "I've stayed away because of the paparazzi and I had to take care of some stuff out of town, but… I'd like to get to know you better, Zoe. And I want to…"

Want to what? Kiss her again? Like she wanted to kiss him?

"Dinner. I want to take you to dinner."

She snarled a soft *grrr*. Of course he wouldn't mention jumping her bones. Tucker was a gentleman. "Tonight?"

"Yes."

"I don't have a babysitter," she blurted. Don's wife, Rosemary, watched the baby when Zoe played in the clubs and the rest was momma and Bugtussle time.

"I have one. Deacon and Quin are going out and taking Noelle with them. Keisha agreed to babysit for us."

Breathless, she asked, "What time?"

"Now?"

Zoe glanced at the black-and-white cartoon cat clock tacked to the wall. "Now?" she squeaked. "It's only three o'clock."

"Well, yeah. But I have a surprise for you and… well…can I come pick you up?"

She calculated how much time she'd have to get ready and tried really hard not to read more into Tucker's invitation. After virtually ignoring her for weeks, here he was asking her out. What was the right thing to do? Her head was adamant. *Don't go down this rabbit hole.* Her heart? Her heart answered before she could think too hard. "Sure."

"See you in about twenty minutes."

Her phone went dead. Zoe was tempted to bang her head on the table. She was now officially, certifiably crazy. Twenty minutes? She squawked, leaped up and charged to the bedroom.

True to his word, Tucker arrived twenty-one minutes later. She'd counted them off as she frantically dressed, fussed with her hair and makeup, and got the baby ready. She was stuffing baby things into the fancy diaper bag when Tucker tapped on the door.

A few minutes later, baby and carrier were strapped into the back seat, and they were off. During the ten-minute drive, Zoe wondered if Tucker considered the condo his home because he didn't seem to spend much time there. Feeling bold, she asked, "Is Nashville home for you?"

Tucker glanced over and she caught his wry grin. "Not exactly. Barron Entertainment owns the town house."

"Then where *is* home?" This was supposed to be a date, right? And he'd said they should get to know each other.

He shrugged, keeping his eyes on traffic. "I have an apartment in the Crown Barron Casino in Las Vegas. I spend most of my time there." He chuckled. "And I still have my room at Mom's, on our ranch near Oklahoma City."

Zoe rolled her eyes and clapped her hands to her chest. "Oh no! A momma's boy."

"Katherine Tate raised seven sons. Trust me, we're *all* momma's boys."

Tucker drove around back, entering through the secured gate to park behind the row of town houses. Keisha was waiting for them. He gestured for Zoe to remain in the car while he dealt with the carrier and diaper bag.

Zoe couldn't stay in the car. She had to get out and give her baby a kiss. "You be good for Keisha, baby boy."

"Little man and I get along just fine. Don't you worry, Zoe. Go have some fun." Keisha's curls danced in the breeze as she laughed. "Have you decided on a name yet?"

Zoe hated to admit that every name she came up with didn't feel—or sound—right. Her brain had wrapped around that whole "Junior" axle and wouldn't let go. She'd mulled over names, discarding most of them. She wondered what Tucker would say if she revealed her thoughts.

The baby cooed up at him and, with a split second of insight, Tucker now totally understood Deacon's reaction to baby Noelle and subsequent feelings for Quin. That wall he'd built between him and Zoe cracked more. He'd never intentionally buttoned up his emotions. He just didn't wear his heart on his sleeve. He wasn't wired that way. Until now, maybe. It was like he'd been living, if not in the dark, then in the shade. This woman and her baby were spreading little rays of sunshine that continuously caught him off guard. There was just something about being with Zoe that warmed him from the inside out.

In answer to Keisha's question, Zoe said, "I was thinkin' about naming him Peter."

Tucker stared at her. "Peter. Peter Parker. Like… Spider-Man?"

"Ohh. That's why the name sounded so familiar."

His jaw dropped, causing Zoe to laugh, and he caught the twinkle in her eyes. "Good one," he admitted, chuckling as well.

"Dillon suggested Rockwell Toppington Parker," Keisha informed them, perfectly straight-faced.

"My brother is—"

Zoe's laughter interrupted him. Giggling, she said, "I could call him Rocky Top for short."

The baby gurgled and kicked his legs. Tucker tightened his hold on the carrier. "Not happenin', little dude," he assured the happy child.

Zoe's expression sobered. "I'm thinking Nashville, because I want to call him Nash for short, but that's kinda stupid. I can't think of any other real name that would work."

"If you want to call him Nash, just name him that. I like it." He flashed her a grin that shaded toward sad, matching the flash of uncertainty he was feeling. "Not that it matters what I think."

Her face softened as she gazed at the baby. "Nash Parker. Plain and simple, like the kind of folks we are." Except she didn't want them to be plain and simple. She had plans. Dreams. She wanted to give her baby the best life she could—one filled with love and happiness and silly fun.

Tucker snorted. "Sugar, there is nothing plain or simple about you in any way, shape or form."

"Nashville Vanderbilt Parker," Zoe blurted out. "And the paperwork's been mailed in. I shoulda kept it simple!"

She looked...not quite panicked. Tucker immediately moved to soothe her. "That's quite a moniker. He'll grow into it."

Still looking uncertain, Zoe asked, "Are you sure it's not…too much?"

He smiled broadly and held out a hand. "We've never been formally introduced. I'm Tucker Cornelius Tate."

Nine

Zoe couldn't help rolling down the window and waving madly. Keisha, holding Nash, stood on a balcony waving goodbye. She felt odd leaving Nash with the Tates' nanny while she went off on a date. Work? No worries. But a date? Okay, it was the whole date thing that had her feeling weird.

As if sensing her mood, Tucker reached over and took her hand, giving it a gentle squeeze. "Why Nashville Vanderbilt Parker?"

She hesitated before answering, fearing her reasoning might sound dumb. "Because he was born in Nashville on the way to Vanderbilt hospital and my last name is Parker."

"And you like the name Nash," Tucker added.

Smiling in relief, she agreed. "And because I like the name Nash."

They rode in a silence that felt companionable but Zoe being Zoe, she had to chatter. "So how come we're startin' this shindig in the middle of the afternoon?"

"You deserve a break. You work hard looking after Nash and singing. I think it's time you get to do something just for you."

"Like what?" Not that she was suspicious or anything.

"Like shopping."

"Shopping? I don't have the mon—"

"But I do." They were stopped at a traffic light and he looked at her again. "You've been traveling light for a long time now, Zoe. You're putting down roots here. And you're working hard. You have a lot of talent, and Don Easley is going to showcase that. You have a unique style and that's part of your image, which goes along with your talent. We're going to hit a store I know of. There will be a personal stylist to handle things so we shouldn't be there too long. Then I'm going to take you out to dinner. We'll be home in time for Nash's bedtime feeding. Hopefully, you'll have had some fun, with the bonus of some new clothes for your wardrobe."

She plucked at a small fray in her denim skirt. Decent clothes would be nice, especially now that she *was* working. He was right about her image. Still, it felt funny to let Tucker pay for it. She began her protest. "Tucker, I don't have—"

He preempted her. "Business, Zoe. Consider this an investment in your career."

"But I don't work for you."

"Not yet." He turned his head just enough for the movement to draw her attention to him. "I want to help. No strings attached."

"I already owe you so much, Tucker." She did a quick calculation of the money she'd stuck into the Pay Tucker Back Fund. She'd managed maybe a hundred dollars. "I've always paid my own way, beholden to no one. It's simpler that way."

He dipped his head toward her and she caught sight of his crooked grin—the one that hinted at a dimple. "I know all about pride, angel. Sometimes you just need to let go and let people help you. You ever heard of a warm fuzzy?" She scowled and he laughed, grabbing her hand and squeezing it. "Let's just say that you're my warm fuzzy. I like tak—helping you out."

Zoe caught the quick shift in wording and wondered what he'd started to say. "I'm not used to people doin' things for me," she muttered.

That got a full-on laugh from him. "Coulda fooled me, darlin'! You're so gracious when anyone tries to do something nice."

She huffed out a breath and leaned away, hoping he'd get the hint. But he didn't let go of her hand. She didn't like the fizzy warmth zinging up her arm from his touch. Nope, didn't like it at all. Much. She sighed inwardly, giving in to what she really wanted to do—keep holding hands with him.

Twenty minutes later, Tucker maneuvered the SUV into a street-side parking space and came around to open her door. He helped her out and maintained a hold on her hand as he led her down the street. She stopped in front of the redbrick storefront and gaped. They were standing in front of the Cumberland Gal Boutique. Nashville's biggest music stars shopped here. She didn't move as Tucker opened the door.

"Zoe?"

"Do you know where we are?" she whispered in a reverent voice. Shopping here was the culmination of just about every fantasy she'd ever had.

"Ah, yeah. Since I drove us here."

"Tucker…" she breathed.

"Zoe…" he teased.

"Hey, y'all!" A perky blonde bounced in their direction. "C'mon in. I'm Marla. You must be Zoe." The young woman stuck out her hand and Zoe shook it. "Mr. Tate gave me an idea of what we're lookin' for today. Y'all just settle over there on that couch, and we'll bring some things out for you to see. Once you've picked out some outfits, we'll go try 'em on."

Tucker led Zoe toward the back of the store; she was so busy rubbernecking at everything she bumped into a table. She caught a stack of sweaters before they toppled and flashed a cheeky grin at Tucker.

"This place…" she murmured. The wooden floor was buffed to a soft patina. Concert posters from country music superstars were painted directly on the exposed brick walls. There were antiques and clothes and boots. Shoes and purses. Jewelry. Everything a gal with any fashion sense at all could want.

A second woman arrived, only slightly less bouncy than the first. "May I get y'all somethin' to drink? We have several nice wines, champagne, a variety of soft drinks, flavored coffees and sweet tea."

Zoe started to decline, but Tucker ordered for them both. "Mocha coffee for Ms. Parker, and I'll take my coffee black. Thanks."

She was reminded once again that Tucker missed very little. Maybe she should have been creeped out from all the stuff he remembered about her but she wasn't. Nope. Not her. She was pleased as all get-out that he knew she liked mustard and horseradish but not mayonnaise. That she liked mocha coffee and café au lait. When she could drink sodas again, it'd be Diet Coke. She liked her beef medium rare, her chicken fried, and the only fish worth eating was fried catfish. Tucker remembered all those things about her—everyday things they'd shared while living under the same roof.

Tucker urged her to sit on a love seat and then joined her. Zoe had been conscious of Marla's assessing looks. Embarrassed by her clothes and overall shape, Zoe plucked at a string unraveling from the hem of her shirt. She felt lumpy and dowdy, especially given the fashionable sales staff and customers.

Their drinks were served and a few moments after that, Marla reappeared with two others in tow, all wrangling hangers. For the next twenty minutes, Zoe was treated to a variety of outfits. Whenever she hesitated before rejecting something, Tucker told Marla to set that item aside. If not for this, she would have had only one thing to try on—a pair of jeans with rhinestones on the pockets. Now, as Marla led her back to a large dressing room, she had skirts and tops, dresses, jeans, more tops and all the accessories—boots, belts, necklaces, bracelets.

Zoe was reluctant to undress because of her post-pregnancy body. Marla ignored her hesitation. "Honey, you look pretty freakin' good for only bein' six weeks past a baby, and you don't even have a personal trainer. I picked out things that'll look good on you. Trust me, okay? This is what I do."

And she did it well, Zoe admitted. There were only two outfits she disliked so much she refused to leave the dressing room to show them to Tucker. The first outfit she modeled was a coral trapeze dress made of chiffon. Sleeveless, it floated down to just above her knees. Paired with a chunky necklace and cowboy boots with lacy cutouts, the dress made her feel almost pretty. Marla suggested a belt matching the boots. It had a large silver buckle set with coral and turquoise. Zoe walked out and the expression on Tucker's face made her want to do a celebration dance right there.

Back in the dressing room, Marla laughed. "I'd say this outfit is a keeper."

Zoe noticed things, too. Whenever Tucker's eyes lit up, that outfit went into the buy pile back in the dressing room. When she'd tried on all the clothes, there were two piles and a bunch of pieces already back on hangers. Those were the rejects and the two assistants removed them without comment. That left her with the "must have" pile and the "maybe" pile, which was at least three times bigger than the "must haves."

Marla handed her the coral dress and accessories.

"You'll want to wear this for your date tonight. I know where Mr. Tate is taking you to dinner. This is perfect."

She changed into the coral chiffon as the piles, including boxes of boots, a few purses and a basketful of accessories all disappeared—as did her skirt, worn boots and the shirt she'd walked in wearing. When she emerged back into the store proper, Tucker was at the cash register. He turned, smiled and held out his hand. Before she could ask, he said, "The store delivers. We're going to dinner. I'm starved."

So was she, but the look on his face? Yeah, she'd seen that look on men's faces before. Tucker Tate looked like he wanted to eat her with a spoon. And dang if that didn't put a smile on her own face.

Romantic. That was Zoe's first thought as they pulled up in front of the historic mansion. A discreet metal sign with gold letters swung from a metal pole. The redbrick house was surrounded by an intricate wrought-iron fence. Black shutters and trim looked dramatic against the weathered brick. The valet handed her out of the passenger seat before hurrying around to the driver's side. Tucker offered his arm—which turned out to be a good thing. Zoe gawked, and paying no attention to her feet, she tripped over a step.

The Rutherford was one of those landmark restaurants, a place famous for food, service and ambiance. Zoe had added it to her bucket list after seeing it in a story on the Entertainment News Channel. She'd heard reservations were impossible and the cost of dining there equaled a week's pay for a singer like her.

She couldn't stop staring as they passed inside. Antique furniture and chandeliers caught her eye, and while she was staring wide-eyed at the walls and ceiling, she hooked the toe of her boot in the beautiful Persian rug cushioning the rich, wooden floors. Once again, Tucker came to her rescue, holding her upright and covering for her by claiming to be the clumsy one.

"So sorry, darlin'. My big feet are always trippin' me up."

As if. The dang man moved like a dancer. Or a boxer. He was all lithe grace and rhythm, each move calculated and sure. He tucked her up close to his side and she pretended not to notice the zing dancing across her skin when he touched her. She also ignored how well she fit under his arm. They should be poster children for "opposites attract" because they were definitely that. It didn't help the way he made her feel, though—all melty inside and craving his kiss. As they followed the dark-suited hostess deeper into the restaurant, she moved ahead of him but Tucker's hand remained on the small of her back, providing a warm connection.

They sat in a little nook with windows overlooking the back gardens and Zoe imagined what it might have been like when this was a house—with a family, and her as the…what? Matriarch? That word put her too much in mind of Etta Smithee and she shivered. She kept waiting for that shoe to drop, surprised it hadn't already. Leave it to Tucker to notice her reaction.

"Are you cold?" Before she could respond, he had his sport coat off and draped over her shoulders. The material carried both his body heat and his scent—a cologne that reminded her of sea spray and sand and blue skies.

Dinner...happened. All of it a blur. The beef melted on her tongue, and she didn't even fuss at the baby vegetables because some sort of tangy sauce had been drizzled over them. The jacket fell away at some point, but she was still surrounded by all things Tucker so she simply surrendered to the magnetic pull he exuded. Emotions she'd stuffed deep inside rose to the surface, and Zoe had to press her lips together to keep from blurting out her feelings. She wanted him. She wanted to be with him. Skin to skin. Heart to heart. A poet would write about their souls soaring into the heavens, joined by a love so eternal that one would not exist without the other.

She burst out laughing. She was such a romantic fool. Tucker wasn't her soul mate. He was just a guy who was mostly nice to a girl down on her luck. He didn't feel her feelings, didn't look at her like she was his only hope of breathing. Except sometimes he did, when no one was looking, when shadows danced over his face. There'd been times when she'd glance up, sometimes when she was holding Nash in her arms, and she'd catch him watching them both, his expression a mix of hunger, longing, tenderness and sorrow—like she and the baby were something he wanted but was convinced he'd never have.

Without thinking, she reached out and touched his cheek. "What are we doin', Tucker?"

"I don't have a flipping clue, angel, but I'm willing to find out. Are you?"

The truth was there on his face. He wanted her in his bed. He didn't have to say it out loud. She wasn't some naive girl blinded by the stars in her eyes. She'd told herself over and over that hooking up with another man was a bad idea, but she couldn't help herself. Didn't want to, in fact, when it came to this man.

Zoe surrendered to her own yearning. "Yeah," she murmured. "I do believe I am."

Ten

Tucker asked the waiter to box up their dessert and passed over his credit card before the bill was brought. His head was full of ideas—all the things he wanted to do to this luscious woman once he got her into bed. He might not wait that long. He could…stop right there. Business and pleasure shouldn't mix. He inhaled in hopes of reining in his thoughts. And decided he didn't care. They both wanted to explore whatever was simmering between them. When she turned to look at him, he smiled. The smile she offered in return went straight to his heart. Yeah, he was in trouble and he planned to enjoy every moment of it.

The waiter returned and Tuck signed the receipt after adding a large tip. As he moved to pull Zoe's chair back from the table, the top of her head collided with

his chin, cracking his teeth together. She flushed, color climbing up her chest to her cheeks. The server had the good sense to duck his head and retreat before laughing. Tuck had to agree. The situation was pretty funny.

"Are you okay?" Zoe asked, rubbing her scalp.

Tucker worked his jaw before saying, "I'm fine. You?"

"Daddy always said I had the hardest head of anyone he knew. Guess he was right." She passed his jacket over and Tuck shrugged into it as Zoe grabbed the gold-foil bag with their boxed desserts. Taking her free hand, he led her toward the front entrance.

The valet saw them coming and darted off to retrieve the SUV. Tucker drew her hand to his mouth and dropped a light kiss on her knuckles. That's when the night exploded with camera flashes and questions.

"Are you and Zoe an item, Tucker?"

"How long have you been together?"

"Is her baby yours?"

Zoe gasped at the horde of reporters. Tucker pulled her behind him and glared. The Rutherford was now officially on his shit list. He and other Nashville celebrities dined here because the place had been discreet, but not anymore.

After Zoe moved to Don's, the media had forgotten about them. This horde had caught him flat-footed.

People blocked the street, and the valet was caught in the crowd. Tucker retreated, urging Zoe back into the restaurant with his body. The hostess had the door open, and she slammed it shut as soon as they were inside.

The manager bustled up, red-faced, wringing his hands and apologizing profusely. He escorted them through the restaurant, into the kitchen and toward the back door. A few moments later, the SUV appeared, backing into the delivery area.

Once in the vehicle, Tucker worked to contain his anger. He wanted to call Bridger and demand security for Zoe. He heard a snuffling sound coming from the passenger seat and tightened his hands on the steering wheel. If those idiots had made Zoe cry…

She pressed one hand to her mouth and her eyes glistened with tears. Tucker leaned closer, trying to decipher the sounds she was making.

"Oh, lord," she huffed out. "I don't think I'm ready for this."

Tucker made sure the area around the condo was clear before he pulled in and parked in the garage. He figured after the incident with the paparazzi, he should gather up the baby and take them to Don's guesthouse. Except he didn't want to do that. He wanted her to stay with him tonight. Wanted both Zoe and Nash under his roof where he knew they were safe. Yeah, he absolutely needed to call Bridger about security.

Keisha met them as the elevator opened onto the living room and gave her "nanny debriefing," as she called it. "Nash had an easy night, and is currently sleeping soundly. He enjoyed his bath, and should be in a dry diaper, though he's had a bottle." Her eyes twinkled as she added, "I also set up a baby monitor."

Before either of them could react, she slipped away, leaving Tucker alone with Zoe.

He couldn't take his eyes off her. As she bent over the borrowed crib, he shed his jacket and draped it over the back of a barstool at the kitchen bar. He couldn't help but peek over her shoulder at the sleeping child. Being this close to Zoe, breathing in her soft cologne made him almost reckless. He cleared his throat as she straightened and turned to look at him. "Do you want to go home?"

She shook her head. "No. Not unless you're ready to get rid of me and Bugtussle here."

Never, he wanted to shout but wisely kept the thought to himself. Tonight was about…what? Seduction? A quick lay? He wanted her, yes. But he wanted her to want him just as much. If they made—no, *when* they made love, it would be a step into the future, one he could never take back.

"I'd like you to stay." When she nodded in assent, he moved away from her, asking, "Would you like something to drink?"

Her shoulder brushed his chest as she faced him, her smile almost shy. "I'm good."

And she was. So very, very good. His hands went to her waist and he leaned down. She very slowly stretched up on her toes, and their lips met. Tuck circled her waist with one arm, supporting her, and pulled her against his body. He deepened the kiss as she opened to him. Her normally nimble fingers sent bolts of pleasure through him as she fumbled with his buttons. "I'll do that," he said, grabbing her hands.

She stepped back as he flicked his shirt open. Zoe watched and licked her lips, giving him all sorts of ideas. He whipped his shirt off and reached, drawing her back. Then he remembered the baby. With only one part of his brain working on logic, he located the monitor and saw it was on. "Upstairs," he murmured as he scooped her into his arms.

Tucker got them into the elevator, got them up a floor, and into the master bedroom. He put her back on her feet and pulled her to him again. Her breasts were full, and even covered by the filmy material of her dress and whatever bra she wore underneath, they felt wonderful pressing against his chest.

He gazed down, his fingers brushing over her bare shoulder. "May I?" he asked, his voice husky.

"Help yourself." Her voice came out raspy, filled with secret promises.

He traced a fingertip along the scooped neckline of her dress while his other hand eased down below her waist to caress her rear. "I've wanted to touch you like this for weeks."

He stroked her breast and forgot about all the reasons he shouldn't do this. He forgot about everything except her—and the idea of seeing her naked. He'd dreamed about the feel of her silky skin, the brush of her hair against his skin. Cupping her face, hc kissed her. As the hot, sweet taste of her filled his mouth, she melted in his arms. He became lost in the texture of her, her scent, her taste. But like a horny teen, he kept waiting to get caught, or for Zoe to change her mind.

For one brief instant, sanity attempted to reassert

itself. This might be a mistake. Seducing her now, like this, edged very close to something off-limits. But temptation won out over good sense.

He tugged the dress away from her shoulder, set his lips on bare skin. Her breath caught and with that quick inhalation, her breasts teased his chest. When her head fell back, he kissed his way toward the throbbing pulse in her throat.

"If you plan to say no, now's the time," he murmured, and bared her other shoulder. "Otherwise, I've got all sorts of plans for you."

"What kind of plans?" She was all but purring now and he buried his nose in the soft skin at the base of her neck.

"Wicked plans. Sexy plans." He fumbled in his pocket and pulled out a condom. "Plans that include this."

Panting, she leaned back just far enough to put a modicum of distance between their bodies. "You got a smoke detector in here?"

Tucker stared at her, nonplussed. "Why?"

A naughty gleam flashed in her eyes. "Because if we keep goin' the way we're goin', we might wanna disable it so the fire department doesn't come to put out the fire we're gonna light."

Laughing, he gave her a smacking kiss with a lot of tongue. This time, he was the one who broke the kiss. "I have a fire extinguisher."

"Good, 'cause you might just have to use it on me."

Still grinning, he laid his lips against hers, the hand at the small of her back dipping to her sweetly rounded butt to pull her closer. Her eyes lit up, and she rocked her hips the moment she encountered his erection.

"I could go seriously crazy over you." Zoe's breathy words teased his mouth.

He kissed and nibbled her lips. When he came up for air, he asked, "Does this have a zipper? The dress, I mean."

"Nope. It's a peel-off."

"Hot damn, my personal favorite." He worked slowly, drawing out the process, the silky material bunching in his hands as he rubbed them up the length of her body. He kept his mouth on hers until they were both trembling. Finally, he drew back and whisked the dress over her head. Then he just looked at her.

She wore a plain white bra with a hint of lace. It was both virginal and the sexiest damn thing he'd ever seen. He wanted to be that bra, cupping her breasts. Her boy-short panties matched, clinging to her full hips and showing him just where to grip her. Zoe's hands, hanging at her sides, fluttered like nervous birds, and she wouldn't meet his gaze.

"I'm trying to think of something memorable to say, but it's really hard when all the blood's drained out of my head."

That got him a nervous laugh, but she said, "Give it a shot."

"Wow."

Her hands fluttered over her belly and her eyes had a pinched look that begged for honesty. "Yeah?"

Tucker pulled her close and kissed her forehead. "Yeah, angel. You're beautiful."

She pushed against his chest and he loosened his embrace. “No I’m not.” She was back to not looking at him.

On impulse, he dropped to his knees, his hands on her sides. He rubbed his thumbs over her skin. Yeah, there were some stretch marks and her belly had this little pooch thing, but seriously? He found it sort of adorable. He’d dated sleek showgirls, fashion models, and there’d been a few actresses, but none of them was as real and sexy as Zoe. Not to him. There was just something about her. He pulled her toward his face and began to kiss his way from one hip bone to the other. If she widened her legs a little, he could taste her. He liked that idea. A lot.

He hooked his fingers in her panties and tugged them down. She was still wearing her cowboy boots and damn if that wasn’t a turn-on, as well. She placed her palm on his head to steady her balance as she lifted first one booted foot, then the other to get her panties off.

“Spread wider, angel," he ordered. She did, and he used his fingers to tease her. She ran her nails across his close-cropped hair as if looking for something to hang on to. He decided she should lie down for this next part.

Standing, he maneuvered her to the bed and pressed her down. She fell back, all but boneless. He knelt and pulled her legs over his shoulders, dipped his head and tasted her. He nipped and kissed, licked and sucked. She was panting and arching against him one moment, and the next, she shattered, and he felt her climax all the way through him. Zoe blinked open her eyes and watched him down the length of her body.

"I like the way you're looking at me," Tucker said.

She flushed, once again a full-body reaction, and he loved it. "Gotta admit, cowboy, I'm kinda enjoying the way you're lookin' back."

He stood and toed off his boots. Moments later, he kicked his feet free of his pants. He liked the way her eyes widened as she caught a glimpse of his erection.

"Is all that just for me?" she teased.

"Absolutely." He stilled as soft burbles sounded from the monitor on the bed. No other noises came. First thing in the morning, he'd turn the guest room into a nursery because he was not nearly done with this woman. Not by a long shot. Tucker kissed her as he rearranged her on the bed, located the condom he'd dropped on the floor and suited up. Zoe's eyes tracked his every movement.

"Like what you see?" He waggled his brows at her.

"Oh yeah," she breathed. "You're even...better than I ever imagined."

"You imagined us like this?"

"Darn straight. I'm a red-blooded country girl. Of course I imagined us doin' the deed."

Tucker laughed. He couldn't help it. He lowered his body until their hips rested together, his erection nestled against her wet heat. Then he buried his face in her hair and breathed deeply. The wavy strands spilled across the couch, like ink on parchment. The scent of ginger and peaches surrounded him, dazzling his senses. Would he ever take another breath and not remember what she smelled like?

Zoe whimpered as she shifted her hips, and then he was sliding into her warm depths. He forgot to breathe for a moment. He pushed up on his elbows, taking most of his weight off her. Her round, firm breasts were large enough to still press against his chest. He withdrew slowly and she tensed, trying to hold him in. He surged into her, then they were in perfect sync.

He faltered when she asked, "What do you see when you look at me like that?"

His sex-fogged brain tried to process the question. How was he looking at her?

"You have this sort of faraway look in your eyes, but you're staring at me like you can't quite figure me out."

Tucker's mouth quirked again. "That's because I can't. Being here with you, like this? It feels so fantastic that I don't want to stop. And trying to think and talk when something feels this good—when *you* feel this good? Angel, that's just plain mean."

She rolled her eyes and laughed, her breath hitching in the middle as he sank all the way into her. "Okay, no more talking. I promise."

And they didn't, because he made sure to kiss her and kept kissing her until they were both panting so hard he had to stop so they could breathe. Hot waves of pleasure rolled through him. He hadn't been kidding when he told her that making love to her felt fantastic.

Zoe kept her eyes open, watching him. She'd never done that. Before, she'd always hoped the guy knew enough to help her get off, had closed her eyes so she didn't have to see the faces he made as he grunted above her. Tucker wasn't like that. She'd already had a big orgasm and a bunch of little ones courtesy of Tucker. The way he filled her, the way he kissed her, the way he *looked* at her. Like he couldn't believe she was there, like she was special—special to him. She wanted Tucker like she'd never wanted any other man. And she was terrified that she'd screw things up. That he'd love her and leave her like every other man, including her father, had done.

She locked her hands around his neck, rocking with his rolling rhythm, feeling tingles in her fingers and toes. This thing between them, it was happening too fast, and not fast enough. Was it real? "I don't care."

Zoe realized she'd said that out loud when Tucker paused and stared down at her, his expression puzzled. "Angel?"

She couldn't remember when he'd first called her that. Somewhere back along the way, but she noticed he never called anyone else angel. Darlin's and sugars and sweethearts aplenty but she was his only angel. She wanted to always feel this way, to have the zings of electricity zapping her skin each time he touched her, the slow build of anticipation as he brought her to the very edge before she plunged over. To have him look at her the way he was now, his eyes soft and so blue they reminded her of the summer sky right before dawn.

She realized in that moment that she could be reckless, could grab the pleasure and the passion Tucker offered, and that he not only would give it all to her, but he'd be there to catch her when she fell. And she would.

Had. Fallen hard. She didn't know what love was, not for sure, but looking up at him, she wanted to find out.

"Do things to me," she pleaded. "Do all those wicked things you promised." *Make* love *to me,* she added silently.

Tucker did. His strong hands fondled and caressed, teased and pleasured her. His mouth devoured hers, and when she could catch her breath, he trailed nips and kisses across her skin. Her heart galloped. Her skin was tight and itchy, like it was going to burst if she didn't come soon. She was so hot she could be running a fever. And still he pumped into her, finding just the right spot inside her, finding just the right spot outside her. He got her right *there,* and she was shaking so hard she thought she might buck him off.

She watched his face, studied the planes and hollows, raised her cheek to rasp along the bristle of his five o'clock shadow. She met his gaze, because he was watching her, too. Those blue eyes of his grew darker and he tensed. He buried his face in her hair, groaning softly as he emptied into her. And then it was glorious for her, too. She didn't shatter. She imploded.

Zoe shook from the aftershocks, chilled and fevered both, as she lay trapped beneath Tucker's body. Was he breathing? Was she? He sucked in a ragged breath and she wanted to laugh, only to discover she didn't have enough air in her lungs. She sucked in a breath, pleased as everything that she'd been the one to do this to him.

"You okay?" he rasped.

"No," she admitted, and felt him stiffen. As he started to roll away, she squeezed her arms around him. “I’m not okay. I’m fantastic.” He relaxed. “What about you?”

“Angel, if you make me come that hard every time we make love, I may not survive.”

She could live with that.

Eleven

Zoe woke up and lay still, listening. Traffic was a faint hum outside the window. She panicked for a minute when she didn't hear Nash breathing. Then she caught the soft, puffing breaths from the monitor. And she remembered. She wasn't in the guesthouse. She was at Tucker's.

She'd been up with Nash every three hours and her eyes felt puffy, like she'd just spent three days sleeping on the beach. Blinking several times, she brought the alarm clock into focus. Nine o'clock. Wow. Nash had slept for over four hours. She stretched until at least half the bones in her body popped, then she punched up the pillows behind her shoulders and stilled, listening once more.

She heard no sounds but those on the monitor. As

luxurious as this place was, the rooms were probably soundproofed. At least she hoped so. Nash had a set of lungs on him, and he'd used them several times through the wee hours of the morning. The first time, she worried Tucker would get mad. He didn't. He was the one who got up, changed Nash, then handed her baby over so she could feed him. He'd disappeared only to return once Nash was full. Tucker explained he'd moved the porta-crib up to the guest room down the hall. He then scooped up the baby and left to put Nash down in his crib. She'd fallen back to sleep almost immediately.

She vaguely remembered Tucker getting up, kissing her goodbye with a murmured, "Have a meeting. Sleep in. I'll be back in time for lunch." As if her stomach was hardwired to her thoughts, it picked that moment to grumble. She wondered how much longer Nash would sleep. Did she have time to grab a shower? Deciding to take a chance, she moved the monitor into the bathroom. She'd hear if he woke up. She could shower, brush her teeth and try to feel—and look—more human.

Thirty minutes later, she found her underwear carefully folded on a chair, her dress draped over the back. Zoe didn't remember picking stuff up last night. Nope, she was too busy enjoying the multiple orgasms. Tucker must have done so before leaving. Was it possible he really was as nice as he seemed?

"Don't look a gift horse in the mouth," she muttered as she slipped on a robe she'd found in the bathroom. She'd dress after taking care of her now very awake child.

Nash was in a happy mood and she cooed at him on the way down in the elevator. The door slid open and she let out a startled scream. Which, of course, startled Nash, who used those magnificent lungs of his to full capacity.

Two women turned to face her and she recognized them immediately. Keisha dashed toward her, apologies falling out of her mouth.

"I told you we should have called first," she scolded Quin, who held a cooing bundle of pink froth. "I'm so sorry, Zoe. Quin and I didn't mean to scare you. Here, let me help."

Before Zoe could resist, Keisha had the carrier and was headed back toward the breakfast bar. "You just sit yourself down. I'll make you some breakfast. I'd offer coffee but you're still breastfeeding. Don't want to introduce this little guy to caffeine quite yet." She tickled the now cooing baby's cheek. "You'd never get him to nap if you do."

Heart still pounding from shock, Zoe eased over to the breakfast bar and stepped up onto an empty stool. Quin laughed and waved a hand. "Don't mind Keisha taking over. Deacon hired her as a nanny but won't let her nanny. She'll use any excuse to snatch children away from their unwary parents so she can cuddle them."

Keisha was whisking eggs and milk in a bowl while waiting for a pat of butter to melt in a small frying pan. "Your husband hired me because I'm writing my doctoral dissertation on the emotional impact of adoption on early childhood development."

Quin rolled her eyes and Zoe found herself smiling. "That, too. Poor Noelle. I hope Deke will have all his emotional baggage sorted by the time we think about having another one of our own." Sliding off her stool with the little girl snugged securely on her hip, Quin sauntered to the fridge and pulled out a bottle of water and a bottle of orange juice. She set them in front of Zoe, then sniffed the air appreciatively. "You didn't mention bacon."

Her mouth watering, Zoe opened the OJ and gulped it down. Her stomach set up a continuous growl, causing her cheeks to redden. Keisha grinned as she dished up scrambled eggs and a plate of fried bacon. "Enjoy."

Quin added, "I trust our baby expert here, even if she tends to go overboard and get all bossy. Keisha has all the degrees in early childhood development. Plus, she likes to cook and insists on doing the grocery shopping."

"Good thing, or this family would starve to death."

"Hey, I can cook."

Keisha slowly turned her head and all but stared down her nose at Quin. "Oh, really?"

"I can make oatmeal." Quin looked defensive. "And tuna salad."

"As long as you don't have to boil the eggs," Keisha teased.

"Hey! That wasn't my fault. Deke distracted me."

Leaning conspiratorially toward Zoe, Keisha stage-whispered, "She left the eggs boiling on the stove and they boiled dry. You ever smelled burnt hard-boiled eggs? I threw the pan away. There was no salvaging it."

Quin tossed a dish towel at the other woman. Keisha caught it with one hand, and Noelle giggled. Zoe was almost jealous of this easy camaraderie. She finished her eggs and chewed on the last piece of bacon. Still hungry, she hesitated to ask for more. When both women leveled their gazes on her, she swallowed down the last bite and braced herself.

"So," Keisha began.

Quin finished, "We haven't had much time to visit. What's your story?"

Aware of how Deacon and Quin met and married from coverage on ENC, Zoe wasn't dumb. She'd had more than her share of interactions with law enforcement. She recognized the other woman's tone of voice. Quin might be sitting there jostling the one-year-old in her lap looking all concerned, but she was all cop at the moment. She concentrated on the bottle of water, taking long, slow swigs to buy time. What had Tucker already told his people? The whole story was a bad soap opera, and a little part of her wanted Deacon Tate's wife to like her—wanted Tucker's sister-in-law to like her. Did she have to tell the whole story, or could she just touch on the most pertinent parts and skate over the rest?

She cleared her throat. "Simple story. I had car trouble and Tucker played white knight. Since we were both headed to Nashville, he gave me a ride."

Quin cut her eyes to Nash. "And the baby's father?"

"Not in the picture." Zoe snapped her mouth shut. She hadn't meant to sound so waspish. At the same time, though she might want these women to like her, they were getting a little too pushy about her past. "Not that it's any of your business."

The smile on Quin's face didn't touch her eyes. "Anything to do with my brothers-in-law is my business. At least you aren't claiming Tucker is the father."

Zoe blinked as her mouth dropped open. "Are you kiddin' me?" She snapped her mouth shut and considered Quin's implication that she might be some gold digger or worse. "Wow. I suppose there are some people nasty enough to do somethin' so low. But that ain't me. Tucker'n me have only known each other a couple of months. He's just a really nice guy with a big heart."

That statement was met with an incredulous look. "We are talking about Tucker Tate, right? The shark of the entertainment world?"

"Well… I don't know about sharks. I do know he drove by, took pity on me and then Nash decided to make an early entrance. Tucker just sorta got caught up in the situation. I appreciate the stuff y'all did for me and Nash after I got out of the hospital. It was really nice an' all, but no offense? This is startin' to get personal. You should go ask Tucker, you wanna know anything else."

"You spent the night. In Tucker's room." Quin was persistent.

"Yes, ma'am, I did. But I don't see how that's any of your business. This is Tucker's house, not yours."

"Tucker doesn't bring strange women here to spend the night."

This was way more information than Zoe wanted to know—even though she was secretly pleased that

Tucker didn't bring just anybody home. But Quin, who had always seemed friendly, still had her cop face on and that made Zoe extremely uncomfortable.

"Thanks for breakfast. I'm sure y'all have way more important things to be doin'." She stood up and looked pointedly toward the front door.

"I'll just clean—"

She cut Keisha off. "You're so sweet, but I can wash the dishes. Thanks kindly for droppin' by."

Quin stood and hitched Noelle on her shoulder, gesturing with a jerk of her head to Keisha. "Guess that's our cue to leave." They headed toward the front door where Quin paused. "A word of advice, Zoe. Tucker is family. I don't like it when anyone messes with mine."

The solid wooden door closed behind the two women with a soft snick that was as much a message as if Quin had slammed it shut. Zoe glanced down at Nash, who was cooing and trying to pull off his socks. "What's she got to be all bent out of shape over? She's the one who came here nosin' around like a bloodhound on the hunt."

Tucker looked up as his office door opened. Deacon walked in, a paper bag in his hand. He kicked the door shut behind him. Deke deposited the bag on Tucker's desk, then went to the sideboard to grab the coffee carafe. He poured himself a cup then refilled Tucker's.

"Dude, seriously? Your wife didn't fix you breakfast?"

His brother rooted around in the bag, pulled out a sugary doughnut and plopped into the guest chair.

"Quin doesn't cook. Keisha did, but it was all healthy and stuff. Besides, it's time for a midmorning snack." Deacon leaned forward and edged the bag toward Tucker. "There's a bear claw in there."

Tuck snatched the bag and looked inside. He'd just taken his first bite when Deacon said, "So…?"

Tuck chewed and swallowed. "So what?"

Deacon let out an exasperated huff. "So…you had a houseguest last night."

"Seriously? You were spying on me?"

"Not true. I had the game on. And I heard noises."

"Uh-huh."

"And you're my brother."

He snickered but didn't reply, sipping his coffee between bites. He settled back. Tuck knew his brother so he waited, in silence. Deke lasted until the end of his doughnut.

"Why are you doing this, little brother?"

"What am I doing, big brother?"

"Don't play dumb. You probably have the most brains of all of us, but if I have to spell it out, I will. What's up with you and Zoe?"

Tucker considered Deacon's question. "I don't know." He held up a hand to stay any protest. "I don't, Deke. It's…new."

"She has talent."

"I know."

Deacon leveled a look at him. "What happens if y'all break up?"

"What do you mean?"

"I mean, she has talent. A lot of it. Talent I want to

help along. If the two of you get together and then you break up with her—"

"Whoa right there," Tuck interrupted. "Why are you automatically assuming I'd be the one to break it off?"

His brother stared at him until he wanted to squirm. Deke finally said, "Seriously?"

Okay, Deacon had a point. Tucker didn't stick with a woman very long, but truthfully, he usually dated only when he needed a plus-one, or if someone really caught his eye. He didn't do relationships. Ever. Until now. He should be rattled by the thought of something long-term with Zoe. Why wasn't he? And that did freak him out. He defaulted to his usual excuse. "Business is business, Deke. I want her to succeed, too."

"Okay, fine. Just don't mess it up. Now tell me how this whole thing started."

So that's just what he did, sparing no detail. And realized he was in even deeper trouble than he thought.

Twelve

Zoe folded the dish towel next to the sink. All signs of her presence upstairs, her visitors and breakfast had been erased. She glanced at her phone to check the time. She could wait until Tucker came home and tell him about the visit from his sister-in-law. She still smarted over Quin's insinuation that she was trying to trap Tucker or something. Or she could call a cab and go back to the Easleys' because she felt funny staying at Tucker's house now. That was probably her best bet.

She gathered up the diaper bag and Nash in the carrier and stepped out the front door. She sat down on the front step to wait. When the cab arrived, she dialed Deacon's number while walking to the street. Keisha answered.

"I'm leaving, and I don't have a key or anything.

Thanks for the loan of the porta-crib and for babysitting. Could you ask Mrs. Tate to lock up and set the alarm?" She clicked off before the nanny could respond.

The cab pulled away as Keisha and Quin appeared. Zoe didn't look back. She got lucky with the cabdriver. He wasn't the nosy type, which was good because she had tears in her eyes. Stupid hormones. She had just enough cash on her to pay the fare with a little extra for a tip. He pulled up at the end of the Easleys' driveway and was gone before she'd taken a few steps after getting out.

For the second time that morning, Zoe let out a startled squeak as a woman, dressed like a professional in a suit with killer heels, stepped out of the bushes.

"Zoe Parker, I presume?"

Zoe eyed her suspiciously. "This is private property."

The woman waved her hand in an airy gesture. "Dandy Don knows I'm here."

Studying her, Zoe considered what to do. She seemed awfully darned familiar with Don. And she looked vaguely familiar. The woman fluttered inch-long eyelashes over blue eyes and brushed a strand of her platinum hair away from her face.

"I'm Parker Grace," the woman announced as if Zoe would automatically recognize the name.

Zoe tightened her grip on Nash's carrier in case she needed to hotfoot it to Mr. Don's house.

"Yeah, and?"

The woman's smile turned predatory, with a hint of

cat eating the canary for spice. Zoe hated her. “I’m a reporter with Entertainment News Channel.”

“Uh-huh.” Zoe turned up the drive and started walking. Mr. Don had warned her about handling the media—as in he’d take care of everything and she wasn’t to talk to them without him there. And he was nowhere to be found. “Well, Miz Grace, that’s real nice an’ all but you aren’t on my schedule today.”

The woman *tsked* at her, but Zoe kept walking. “I believe you’ll want to talk to me. Especially since you spent the night with Tucker Tate.”

Zoe’s step faltered but she caught herself and kept going. How the heck did this reporter know that?

“I’m sure you’re aware that the Tates and the Barrons are two of the richest families in the country.”

“So?” Zoe hoped her shrug and “whatever” expression would give the woman a clue. She hadn’t realized how long this driveway was and since the reporter continued to dog her, Zoe wondered how she would get inside the guesthouse without a hassle. She glanced up the drive but didn’t see either Mr. Don’s or Miz Rosemary’s cars.

“You really should agree to an interview, Zoe. I know all about these people from personal experience.” The woman grabbed for her arm.

Was this Parker Grace person threatening her? Zoe wished Mr. Don was here. Heck, she’d even settle for Tucker. All she knew was that she was tired, Nash was fussing and needed to be fed, and this woman had invaded her space. She hooked the carrier over her elbow, fished her phone out of the diaper bag and dialed 911, swiping the speaker button as the call rang through.

A recorded voice answered, "Nine one one, what is the exact location of your emergency?"

"Yes, hi. This is Zoe Parker. I'm stayin' with the Easleys on Valley Brook just off Woodmont. They aren't here and this woman confronted me an' my baby in the driveway."

Parker fisted her hands on her hips, her face looking so hard Zoe was afraid it might crack when she spoke. "Fine. I'm leaving. But don't say I didn't warn you, Zoe."

Zoe grabbed Nash's carrier and scuttled up the driveway, keeping an eye on the reporter. If she'd been alone, she might have duked it out with the woman right there, but she couldn't do things like that anymore. Because of Nash. The woman sauntered away, a taunting smile on her face. "Don't get your hopes up, little girl. Men like Tucker Tate eat starry-eyed wannabes like you for breakfast." She flicked a card that landed in the baby carrier. "Call me when you grow up and want to talk."

"Hello?" a live 911 operator said into the sudden silence. "Are you there?"

Zoe stared at the phone a long moment before replying. "I'm sorry. Yeah, I'm here."

"What's happening? I have a patrol car headed your way, but I need the exact address."

"Thank you, but you can probably tell them they can go on about their regular business. The woman who confronted me is gone now."

"Are you sure you're safe?"

"Yessum. Turns out she was just one of those gossip reporter people. She mistook me for someone else. S'all good. I'm sorry to have troubled you."

"Zoe," the operator's voice was full of compassion. "If someone is still there and you feel you can't talk—"

"No, ma'am. She left." Zoe glanced at the card. She didn't want any trouble, especially not after her little confrontation with Tucker's sister-in-law, but she didn't like Parker Grace either. "She said her name was Parker Grace and claimed to be a reporter with ENC."

The dispatcher sucked in a breath. "I've heard of her. Are you sure you'll be okay?"

Nash chose that moment to wail. He was probably wet and hungry. "Yes, ma'am. Thank you kindly. I need to look after my baby now." She soothed Nash as she walked. First, all those photographers at the restaurant last night, and now this Parker Grace lady—Zoe snorted. *Lady* might be a stretch. Having a reporter trespass on the Easleys' property made her nervous. She should call Tucker, tell him about the incident, but she worried. Would Tucker get mad at her? Think she'd done it on purpose, lookin' for publicity? Since nothing had happened, maybe she'd just keep it to herself.

Tucker clicked off the call and immediately redialed. The phone on the other end rang and rang. Just like it had the first time. Zoe always answered. Had something happened to her? To Nash? Or maybe she'd taken off for parts unknown?

Bent Star's administrative assistant, a no-nonsense

woman with a tendency to mother, stood as he passed her desk. "Tucker? What's wrong?"

"Nothing. Everything. I don't know, Patty. Zoe isn't answering the phone." He trotted down the hall, the woman dogging his steps.

"Are you calling her cell phone?"

"Yes."

"Where is she? Is she still at the Easleys'?"

He glanced back at her, and huffed out a breath, confessing, "I left her asleep at the town house."

"Call the house phone. Maybe she's down in the kitchen or something, left her cell upstairs." Patty favored him with her "wise mother" look. "I've never seen you quite so frazzled." She left off the implied *over a woman.*

"You'll feel better if you go check on her. Take her to lunch. Your schedule is clear. Spend the afternoon with her. And if you need a babysitter, call me." She gave him a gentle shove and a knowing smile.

Deciding to take Patty's advice, Tucker reached the front door of Bent Star's offices, only to be hailed by his brother.

"Yo, Tuck. You headed home? Can I catch a ride?"

Tucker kept walking. "Yes, and why?"

"Spending time with one of my favorite brothers isn't reason enough?"

Tuck snorted and kept walking. So did Deke. Tucker drove the company SUV since he had the keys. It was a short trip and Tucker made mental bets on how long it would take for Deke to open up. He hadn't anticipated the answer to be immediately.

"So… I couldn't help overhearing that you can't get in touch with Zoe."

"Uh-huh. Do you know something about that?"

"Quin called me a little bit ago."

Tucker cut his eyes to his passenger, as he braked and the SUV rolled to a stop at a light. "And?"

"Well… She and Keisha went over to see Zoe this morning."

Now he turned his head to stare at Deke. "I'm not going to like this, am I?"

Deke scrunched up his face, trying to look both apologetic and brotherly. "Probably not. Quin didn't come right out and say that she'd interrogated Zoe but given her rant over the girl's reaction to—" he made air quotes "—'a few friendly questions about her background,' I don't think it went well."

Tucker growled but returned his eyes to the road when the car behind them honked because the light had turned green. "What did your wife do, Deacon?"

A long sigh answered the question. "She sort of called in a favor and ran a background check."

Furious, Tucker hit his blinker and whipped the big SUV over to the side of the street. Throwing the transmission into Park, he turned on his brother. "Dammit, Deacon—"

Deke held his hands up, palms facing Tucker as he cringed back against the passenger door. "I know. I had strong words with her. And I'm probably looking at a fight when I get home. She was totally out of line, but—"

"But what, Deke? You think I didn't have Bridge

check? Nash's father is serving a life sentence for murder. Zoe's father died in a county jail, most likely of cirrhosis of the liver. She's dirt-poor, a single mother and wants to sing for a living. What the hell can you or that snoopy wife of yours tell me that I don't already know and haven't already thought?" He snarled and banged his hands on the steering wheel, surprised at both his anger and the hollow feeling growing in his gut. What if Zoe had packed up Nash and left? They could be anywhere. Except… She didn't have much money. "I ought to make you get out and walk home."

Muttering imprecations under his breath, Tucker slammed the transmission into Drive and managed to merge back into the midday traffic.

He growled again when Deke continued. "Zoe and the baby left in a cab. About thirty minutes after Quin and Keisha went home. She called Keisha to tell them to lock up the town house since she didn't have a key." As much as Tucker wanted to ditch Deacon, he didn't have time and maybe having his brother grovel on behalf of his wife would help smooth things over with Zoe. He changed their course, heading for the Easleys' estate. He remained silent for the rest of the drive. So did Deke. When Tucker finally pulled up the driveway and parked, he was calm enough to speak without cussing.

"You tell Quin to stay out of my business, Deke. And she's not to go near Zoe again. Tell her to pass on that message to the Bee Dubyas. I don't want any interference from them. We clear on this?"

His brother huffed out another long-suffering sigh. “They care, bud. We all do.”

“Yeah? What about Zoe? Do you care about what happens to her? To her baby?”

Deacon’s quiet reply didn’t come until Tucker opened the door and was halfway out of the SUV. “Not as much as we care about you.”

Thirteen

Zoe moved the porta-crib out to the gazebo next to the pool. Nash was down for his nap so Zoe ate the lunch she'd heated in the microwave—tomato soup along with two pieces of cheese slapped between slices of bread. Not exactly a grilled cheese sandwich but it was gooey. She did her best to ignore the hollow spot inside her that no amount of food would ever fill up. She'd let her pride—and her insecurity—get away from her. Of course Deacon's wife would want to know about her. The woman had been a highway patrol trooper—she still was for all Zoe knew. And they had a baby girl. Like that reporter said, the family was rich. Zoe could have been just what Quin said. She could have been a thief. Or worse.

She wasn't. Still, the fact they didn't trust her hurt

on a level so primal she couldn't wrap her head around the sick, empty feeling it caused. She pushed the bowl and plate aside, her appetite gone. Nash was still napping so she unpacked her guitar, pulled out her notebook and settled in to play. She often played and sang to him while he slept.

Though her fingers plucked the guitar strings, her brain didn't focus on music. She'd been an idiot to think there might be something between her and Tucker. They were worlds apart, the gulf so wide that one night of mind-blowing sex wouldn't bridge it.

One thing Zoe had always been was honest with herself. She was country roads and Tucker was straight-up city lights. No matter how hard she imagined it, Tucker would remain a dream she couldn't quite reach. Not at this point in her life. Maybe when she got famous—if she got famous. She'd make a life for Nash, one way or another—a better one where he would grow up to be whatever he wanted to be.

She stared out across the wooded backyard, eyes unfocused. She'd discovered that the gazebo was a good location for songwriting—the breeze blowing gently, dappled sunlight, birds chirping, the occasional squirrel darting playfully across the lawn. And it was just her and Nash. This was a cozy place. Peaceful.

Zoe played a riff on the guitar, trying out different chord progressions until she found a tune she liked. Playing it over and over until she had it memorized, she stopped to make notations in her book. Then she played the tune again, humming along. Her thoughts returned to Tucker, to the daydreams she'd had of lazy mornings as he lingered over coffee before leaving to go conquer the world, to late nights curled up in his bed after coming home from her current singing gig before making sweet love.

Tucker was handsome enough to be a matinee idol. She smiled at the old-fashioned term. There'd been an old lady who lived next door to her and her daddy at some point. She dyed her hair blue and swore that she'd been kissed by Clark Gable when she was a giddy girl of eighteen. At the time, Zoe had no idea who Clark Gable was. She'd crept into the local library and looked him up. That was the summer she discovered she could check out movies if she had a library card. She dragged her dad down there to sign for her and then she found a cheap VHS player at the pawnshop. She swept the floors and cleaned the bathrooms for two months in trade for it. That was her introduction to Clark Gable, Humphrey Bogart, John Wayne. She'd wanted to be as strong as Lauren Bacall, as intelligent and witty as Katherine Hepburn and as beautiful as Grace Kelly when she grew up.

She hummed the first line and then sang, "You can't be the hero." A few more chords and the chorus came to her almost whole. Then she put everything together. "You can't be the hero, not in my story. You aren't the kind of man who would ever share the glory. You won't ever love me. We just can't be."

Zoe leaned over to write down the words and to change one of the chords, then she played and sang the chorus again. No more words came so she just stared at the garden. Storm clouds gathered overhead and within moments, the sun's light was muted, washed in somber grays. She knew how the sun felt. And it sucked.

She closed her eyes, wrapping the feeling around her, then jotted down the words as they came to her.

I'm not lookin' for true love,
'Cause I'll just find a broken heart.
But when I look at you,
I want to give you everything.

She strummed the chords, found the key and sang them. Then she added the chorus. She didn't fight the melancholy. This was her reality. Tucker Tate was so far above her. Someday, maybe. If her dreams came true, then yeah. She might be able to walk up to him as an equal. And just like that, the second verse came to her. Zoe captured the words then sang them.

You can't be the one for me,
No matter how hard I wish it.
But when you look at me,
I want to give you everything.

Deke grabbed his arm as they approached the guesthouse, effectively stopping him in his tracks. Tucker gave him a hard look and then he heard the music floating on the breeze. Deke held his finger to his lips, cautioning Tuck to be quiet. His brother obviously wanted to listen without Zoe knowing they were there.

He was smart enough to know he wasn't as good a judge of talent as Deke and Chase were. His forte was the business side of things, but there was just something about Zoe that pricked his senses. Her voice resonated like a young Dolly Parton's, only deeper, huskier. When Zoe sang a love song, a man felt it deep inside, and it put thoughts of rumpled sheets and sweaty sex in his brain. His upper lip curled into an unconscious snarl. He'd need to check with Deke and Dillon about what thoughts Zoe put into their heads. He wasn't sure he liked the idea of a bunch of fans thinking what he was whenever Zoe got up onstage.

He caught whispers of her guitar and remained still. Yes, he fully intended on eavesdropping because he was as intrigued as Deke. They stood just out of sight.

"You can't be the hero," she sang, voice low and sweet. "Not in my story. You aren't the kind of man who would ever share the glory. You won't ever love me. We just can't be." Her voice grew husky, then cracked on the word *can't* and Tucker's heart cracked a little, too. There was so much loneliness in the words. And hurt. Was she singing about Redmond Smithee? He wanted to beat the hell out of him. The man had been a cretin to throw away this wonderful woman and her child.

It took conscious effort on his part to unclench his hands. Part of him wanted to burst around the corner, sweep Zoe into his arms and kiss her until she wasn't lonely anymore. The rational part leaned against the guesthouse wall and considered the situation. Tucker wasn't a protector. That was Hunter and Bridger. He wasn't the strong, silent type. That was Cooper. Deacon and Dillon were the sensitive types—while still keeping their man cards. Boone? He had brains and mad organizational skills. Hunt called him a dog robber, a term from his oldest brother's military days describing someone who expedited things. Need something or want something done? Ask Boone. He could find anything, and he made things happen. Him? Tucker wrinkled his forehead. He understood numbers. Business. Profit and loss. He didn't do feelings—not really. He wasn't cold. He loved his mother, brothers, cousins and their wives—most of the time.

That said, he'd never been in love. Heck, he'd never gone steady—not in high school, not in college. Tucker had never loved a woman he wasn't related to and from his current perspective? That just sucked, especially given the woman sitting in the gazebo. He'd wanted to wake up next to her that morning, share coffee with her, breakfast. But he'd had a meeting at the office—one that couldn't be canceled. So he'd gone, albeit reluctantly. And then Quin stuck her nose in, and now things were awkward at best, more likely totally screwed up.

The irrational part of his brain insisting he go gather Zoe into his lap and hold her was squashed by the logical part that decreed he sneak away, then return making a lot of noise to announce his arrival. *Then* he would sweep her into his lap and hold her. He almost snorted out a laugh at that thought.

Deke flashed him a look and jerked him back toward the driveway, and they walked far enough away she wouldn't overhear their conversation.

"Why didn't you tell me she was a songwriter?" Deke hissed at him.

Favoring his brother with a confused look, Tucker said, "I had no clue."

"Well, I'm tellin' you, we need to lock her into a contract, bro, and it needs to be done before you do something stupid to mess up your relationship."

"We don't have a relationship." Of course, after last night, he should probably reconsider that denial. He stabbed a finger toward Deke. "And wasn't your wife the one who scared Zoe off this morning?"

Deacon had the good grace to look sheepish. "I said I'd talk to Quin." Tucker held up a warning finger. "And the Bee Dubyas," Deke finished with a disgruntled huff. "Get with Don and get her signed, Tuck. You sit her down with Dillon? I can name five female singers who would catfight over recording that song. Heck, *I'd* record it, but it's not written for a man." Deacon hooked his thumbs in his pockets and stared at Tucker. "You know, our opening act is taking a break."

Tucker had been staring at the pool. "Wait. What? Sugar Tree? What's up with them?"

"Something to do with family. It's college venues until we hit Talladega in two weeks. We planned to play solo. But, dude, I'm walking up to that gazebo and asking Zoe to come on the road to open for us. You'd best work a deal with Dandy Don." Deke turned to retrace his steps, but Tucker snagged his arm, holding him in place.

"She can't go on tour. What about the baby?"

Deke shrugged. "Quin's taking some vacation time. She, Noelle and Keisha are coming with me. Keisha can look after both kids."

"How's that going to work since Zoe and Quin aren't exactly best friends at the moment?" Tucker did *not* like the idea of Zoe and Nash out on the road somewhere. Away from him. He put his brain on hold. Why should it matter? Just business, right?

"Good point. We'll lease a tour bus for her. She and Nash will stay in it and Keisha will watch him when Zoe's performing."

Tucker folded his arms over his chest and scowled. "Sounds like you have this all planned out."

Rolling his eyes, Deacon wasn't intimidated in the slightest. "Look at it this way. It'll give you a chance to take her shopping again. She'll need outfits to perform in."

"And who's paying for them? She's already plotting how to pay me back for what I spent on her yesterday." Still, Tucker grinned, remembering when he'd taken his cousin Chase Barron's new bride shopping in Las Vegas. A Choctaw cowgirl, Savannah had been the Western version of Eliza Doolittle, and Tucker had played Professor Henry Higgins, without the romantic bits. He'd reinvented the rodeo rider so she could hold her own against Chase's demanding family.

"Work a deal with Dandy Don. Tell her it's an advance on her earnings. We leave in two days. You need to get a contract drawn up and get on this, bud."

Numbers, Tucker reminded himself. The bottom line. That's what he was good at. And it was time to show Zoe Parker just what she could be. With that in mind and making logistical plans, he followed Deke to the gazebo.

Deke called out as soon as they turned the corner. "Yo, Zoe! You got company, girl."

She scrambled to hide a notebook under her guitar in its battered case, then she stood. Tucker took in the off-the-shoulder drape of her oversize T-shirt and the tight jeans molding their denim to her lush curves. The memory of everything they'd done the previous night rushed to the front of his brain.

She was too busy scowling at Deacon to notice him, though. "I'm not sure I want your company at the moment," she finally said.

Fourteen

Zoe almost laughed—almost. Watching both men grovel was a sight to behold. The thing was, she believed they were sincere. Deacon looked and sounded contrite and apologetic for his wife's insinuations. Tucker? Tucker was downright angry on Zoe's behalf. When Nash woke up crying, it was Tucker who moved to pick him up. She wasn't quite sure how to process that. Both men moved toward the baby, but Tucker was quicker. Of the two, she'd figured Deacon had more experience, since he was a daddy and all. Then again, he did have a nanny. All Zoe's preconceived notions were being blown out of the water.

"He's wet," Deacon announced, utterly positive.

"I'll change him," Tucker said. "You explain to Zoe what you have in mind and tell her to call Dandy Don."

Call Mr. Don? Zoe sank onto the cushioned patio chair and eyed Deacon suspiciously. "What's goin' on?"

Deacon dropped into the chair across from her and stretched out his long legs. Zoe pushed her chair back and propped her feet in the chair between them, her boots sticking out like stop signs.

"Are you aware that Sugar Tree has been opening for me on this tour?"

She nodded. Sugar Tree was an up-and-coming female duo and they'd hit the jackpot when they got the Red, White and Cool tour gig.

"They've had to take a hiatus for a few weeks. I'd like you to fill in for them."

She blinked. Tilted her head. Blinked again, then scrunched her face up in concentration as she processed what he'd just said. Then thoughts tumbled through her brain like dominoes in one of those YouTube videos. How could she tour with Nash? Who would look after him? Was she ready for that kind of gig? Would she be expected to stay with the band on their bus? Her brain circled the drain. What would she do with Nash?

Deacon reached over and patted her boots to get her attention. "Breathe, Zoe. It's okay. You'll need to call Dandy Don, but here's what I'm thinking. We'll lease an RV, provide a driver. Quin and Noelle are coming with me so that means Keisha, too. She can look after Nash when you're performing. It's a few weeks, but good exposure for you and money in your pocket. What do you think?"

She didn't hide her scowl. "Question is, what does your wife think?"

Deacon winced but it was Tucker, still holding Nash, who spoke. "I'll go with you to run interference in case there's a problem. What do you say?"

Zoe answered before she thought things all the way through. "Yes!"

Tucker climbed down from the corporate jet at the Morgantown Municipal Airport, his angry strides quickly eating up the distance from the plane to the terminal. He'd been called to Barron Tower in Oklahoma City for a huge strategy meeting. Someone was screwing with Barron Enterprises, which meant they were messing with the family. It turned out the troubles in Vegas were just the beginning. He hadn't planned to be gone from the tour for four days. He was so mad at his brother—and himself, truth be told.

The call had come at 4:00 a.m. that morning. Zoe. Sounding lost and scared. The driver hired for her bus was drunk and weaving all over the road.

Grim-faced, Tucker brushed past people in the terminal and headed outside. A taxi awaited him. He climbed in and clenched his jaw shut to keep from yelling at the driver to go faster.

Idiot, he berated himself. Who had vetted the driver for Zoe? He'd damn sure find out and then heads would roll. He'd stayed on the phone with her while he called his lame excuse for a brother from a different phone and rousted his butt out of bed. And he'd talked to her until the buses stopped, and she and Nash transferred to Deke's personal bus. The driver was arrested by highway patrol.

And then he'd called for the corporate jet. Now he was only a few minutes away from her. And he needed to calm the hell down. Before he took a swing at his brother. Because it wasn't Deacon's fault. And he couldn't be angry at the Barrons for keeping him away. The family was under siege and he had a responsibility to do his part. But Zoe had been alone. With a drunk driving her and the baby. Something could have happened. He could have lost them. And he didn't like that thought one bit.

The cab rolled to a smooth stop at the cluster of sleek RVs. He stuffed a couple of twenties through the plastic barrier and got out. The door on the newest RV, commissioned by Deacon when he married Quin and they adopted Noelle, popped open. He was expecting to see Deke. He got his sister-in-law instead.

"Don't start, Tucker," she preempted. "You won't be saying anything we haven't already."

He scrunched his brows and glowered at her, surprised. "Deke promised to look after her."

"It's not Deke's responsibility."

"You're really gonna go there?" He was still annoyed with her for the way she'd treated Zoe back in Nashville. "Where is she?"

Quin shrugged. "Once we got here, she went back to her bus. We asked her to stay."

Tuck backed up a step. "We? Like she'd stay with someone who accused her of...what, Quin? Being poor? Of working her tail off? Of having dreams *above her station*?" That last bit was so coated in sarcasm he could taste it on his tongue. "She's never been given a thing in her life. All she has is her pride, her talent and sheer stubbornness." He shook his head. "You of all people, Quin, should have some degree of sympathy for her. Tell Deke we'll talk later. Alone."

He pivoted and headed toward Zoe's RV. When Quin called after him, he simply held up a hand, gesturing to leave him alone. As he reached the RV's door, it swung open. One of the roadies stuck his head out, nodded and climbed down with a quiet, "Zoe and the kid are fine."

Tucker wouldn't take the guy's word for it. He had to assure himself that Zoe and Nash were okay. He slipped inside and heard Nash gurgling happily but no response from Zoe.

When he arrived at the bedroom area, Nash held up his arms and cooed. Zoe looked ragged, dark circles under her eyes so large her eyelashes couldn't disguise them. He scooped up the baby, located the diaper bag and took the kid into the living area. He put Nash in a fresh diaper, then found a baby bottle in the little fridge and settled in.

The next thing Tucker knew, he must have dozed off on the couch, with Nash on his chest. Zoe's soft laughter woke him.

"Thanks for lettin' me sleep in," she murmured.

"You had a rough night." He carefully maneuvered until he was sitting upright, the baby now cradled on his shoulder.

Zoe bustled around the kitchen area fixing coffee,

which got her a raised eyebrow from him. "I called his pediatrician before I left Nashville. He said switchin' Bugtussle to formula full-time at this point isn't a big deal. So I did. Easier on both of us, I think."

When the coffee maker stopped dripping, she poured Tucker a cup—black. She mixed creamer and sugar into hers and joined him on the couch. "Wasn't expectin' you to drop everything and come."

"I'm just sorry I wasn't here. I'll be around now."

She blinked rapidly, and was that a glint of moisture in her eyes? "But you're..."

"I'm what, angel?"

"A busy man. You've got all those companies to see to, and...and..."

"Shh. It's not like I have to be in an office every day." He should be but he couldn't get Zoe out of his head and being apart from her—and Nash—made him all kinds of crazy.

He leaned over and kissed her, whispering against her lips. "I'm never too busy for this."

Zoe stood in the middle of the large stage filling one end of the West Virginia University Coliseum. She'd just finished singing "Take Me Home, Country Roads" and the place had erupted. She always sang unaccompanied until the last song of her set. In Tuscaloosa, at the University of Alabama, she'd owned the crowd the moment she played the opening notes of Lynyrd Skynyrd's "Sweet Home Alabama." In Lexington, it was "My Old Kentucky Home." And each time, halfway through the last song, the Sons of Nashville joined in, behind her in the dark. Then Deacon would walk out and join her, to new applause, whistles and shouts.

"Zoe Parker," Deke announced when the song was over, and her name echoed through the huge space, rising above the frantic noise. Then Deke was in the spotlight and she was scrambling offstage, to be met by a grinning Tucker.

Resisting the urge to run into his arms, she slung her guitar behind her and fisted one hand on her hip. "And just what do you think you're lookin' at, mister?"

"You, angel. I'm looking at you."

She waggled a finger. "Don't start that romance stuff with me."

Tucker stepped to her, grabbed the finger and brought it to his mouth. "You don't like romance? Cool. We can get straight to things then."

Cocking her head to study him, she considered his expression. There was heat in his eyes as they roamed over her body. Heat and hunger. This man wanted her. A whole lot. "Nuh-uh. I'm hungry."

"Fancy that. Me, too."

She waved her hands at him like she was shooing chickens and backed up a couple of steps. She needed space and air because the way he was looking at her? She was about to combust. "Not that kind of hungry," she managed to say, though her voice came out husky and needy. "Food. Real food. Greenroom food."

"We'll get it to go."

He snagged her hand and pulled her through a gloomy corridor toward the room that had been set up for the stars to relax in. She filled a plate with bread, cold cuts and cheese, fruit and cookies. Tucker followed, filling a plate with the exact things she put on her own. She tossed him a narrow-eyed look.

"I figure you'll want to eat the leftovers tomorrow while we're traveling."

How did he know? She eyed the bottles of water, sodas and energy drinks. Her hands were full, and her guitar was still slung over her back. Tucker snatched the plate from her hands. "Whatever you think needs to get done, do it now. Then tell me what drinks you want. I'll put them in my pockets."

"Are you reading my mind?"

"No. I just know how that mind works."

Five minutes later, they were crossing the crowded parking lot to the area where the tour buses had been cordoned off with sawhorses and road barriers. Inside her RV, he indicated she should eat while he put everything else in the fridge. He glanced at the watch on his wrist. "We have two hours. Eat fast."

She laughed. "But you just said we have two hours."

He growled low in his throat and stalked to her. "We have two hours. I don't intend to stand here and watch you eat the entire time. I have far sexier things in mind." He eased the shirt off her shoulders and stared at her bared skin. Zoe fought the shiver his gaze elicited but it won. When he skimmed his lips over her neck and shoulder, she moaned.

"Eat fast, angel."

A ball of lust curled in her belly and she forgot she was hungry. For food. Her hunger for Tucker? It exploded. She lifted her chin and tilted her head to give him more room. “You need to stop that.”

“Not a chance. Eat faster.”

She gulped and despite the tiny rumble her stomach emitted, she was sure she couldn’t take a bite, much less chew and swallow.

“You have five minutes. Then I’m stripping you down and eating what I’m hungry for.” His voice came out in a purr as he rubbed his lips over her skin.

“I’m not hungry now.”

He said nothing, but his hand moved to cup her breast. His thumb and finger found her nipple and played with it through the material of her shirt and bra.

“Tucker?” Goodness. Was she sounding breathless again?

“Mmm?”

“Did you hear me?”

His gaze lifted to hers, and she tumbled into blue eyes the color of a hot summer sky. Nerves fluttered in her stomach. No way would she be able to eat now. “We better put this in the fridge.”

“*Mmm.*” He licked up the side of her neck.

“I’m not kidding, Tucker.”

“Neither am I.” He grabbed the plate and shoved it in the fridge, then swiveled and leaned forward so he could grip her hips. He slid her toward him, and once her legs cleared the table, he hitched her up. Her legs wrapped around his waist in self-preservation. “Are you ready for this?”

Was there any way to be ready for the intensity of this man? He backed unerringly down the length of the RV, turned when his knees hit the bed and crawled onto it with her still clutching him.

Swamped by the heat of him, by the scent of his expensive aftershave that reminded her of sand and sea and wind, she clamped around him. If she didn't hold on, she might rocket off into the night. He was kissing her now, taking her mouth, owning it. Now his mouth was on her breast. When had he taken off her shirt? "Hold on," she murmured. "Hold on tight."

"You do that, angel," Tucker whispered into her ear.

His hands and mouth were everywhere. So many sensations bombarded her, she could barely catch her breath. Her skin was hot, tight, like she might burst out of it if he kept touching her. Then she was naked, but that didn't help. She wanted something. Something… more. His fingers teased between her legs. *Yes. Yes, there.* She squirmed but he held her still with an arm across her hips. And then he was inside her and the pressure built and built and built. Quivering, shaking, unable to breathe, she came with a scream that he caught with a kiss.

Tucker's hands were rough yet tender as he petted and smoothed and eased her down from her orgasm. She was staggered by the intensity of it. Then she realized he was still dressed. She glanced down. He'd done that to her with just his mouth and fingers? Torn between anger and amazement, she tugged at his shirt. She wanted flesh. His. Her lips on his skin. Her hands on him. Her mouth. She fumbled with his belt.

"Here, angel, let me."

No, no, no. She had to do this. "No. Me." She pushed

against his right side with her thigh, rolled him to his back and straddled him. She had to hurry. She wanted him—*all* of him—inside her. She needed to touch him, taste him. She inhaled, his scent filling her senses again, only now there was a fragrant musk along with the sea and sand. She got his belt undone, his zipper down, but his jeans stuck. Frustrated, she jerked and pulled.

"Easy, baby, easy," Tucker soothed. "We've got time. Hang on. Just hang on a minute." He lifted her off him, much to her consternation, but only long enough to kick off his boots, slither out of his jeans and briefs, and dig out a condom. Then she was flat on her back, legs wide, as he settled between them. "You can ride me later, sweet girl," he murmured into her hair.

She shuddered beneath him, rolling her hips against his hard length. She reached out and closed her hand over him, lined him up and accepted all of him inside her. She wanted him buried so deep that they would be joined together always. She knew that it was wrong. That he wasn't the man who could love her. It wasn't possible, but she'd already torn through the boundary of good sense. She couldn't go back now, no matter how badly her heart would shatter when the end came. And it would. It always did. But she had the here and now with him. It would have to be enough.

Pleasure saturated every cell of her body as he plunged into her, driving over and over as she arched her hips to meet his thrusts. She watched his clear, blue eyes blur with his arousal and desire. She felt his muscles tense as he throbbed inside her and then he was coming and coming hard, a moan escaping from deep in his throat. And he was hers. For this moment—even if this was the only time she would have with him, for this moment, he was hers.

She swallowed the sudden surge of saliva in her mouth and watched Tucker watch her throat work. His eyes shaded into sapphire territory. Good lord, but she was in so much trouble when it came to this man. She craved him like a dying man craved salvation. Oh yeah, this man was her salvation and her damnation all at the same time. She couldn't have Tucker Tate, not in the long run, because he *was* Tucker Tate, richest of the rich tycoons, and she was Zoe Parker, a free spirit with a beat-up Gibson guitar and a brand-new baby. She was most definitely *not* the type of woman a man like Tucker would hook up with—not for the long haul. But she wanted him, for as long as she could have him. She only hoped that when the time came, she and Nash would be okay.

Zoe startled when Tucker stroked her cheek with the back of his knuckle. "Hey, angel. What put that sad look on your face?"

And then the tears, as sure as rain in April, started dribbling down her cheeks. Strong arms gathered her close and a warm hand rubbed her back. "I am such a mess," she blubbered, trying to push away so she could hide her embarrassment.

"Shh, Zoe. I'm not going anywhere and neither are you. Now tell me what's wrong."

He continued murmuring comforting things to her, most of which she tuned out, content just to be held. She couldn't remember the last time a man held her like this, the last time she felt safe and protected. Not even when her daddy was alive.

She didn't answer him, afraid she'd spill everything—all her hopes, her dreams, her feelings for him—if she opened her mouth. She evened out her breathing, closed her eyes, pretended to sleep, waiting for him to do the same.

"Men like you don't fall in love with girls like me," she finally said.

"Sometimes we do," Tucker murmured into her hair.

Fifteen

"Tucker!"

When the convoy stopped for lunch at a huge travel center, Tucker waited outside by Zoe's RV, talking to the replacement driver. Zoe went into the rest stop to buy snacks.

Now she was flying across the travel stop's apron, Nash on one hip, flapping a tabloid in her other hand. A clerk chased after her.

Tucker met her halfway and held his hand up to the clerk as he tried to make sense of Zoe's babbling. She finally thrust the paper at him, and he snatched it before it blew away.

"She didn't pay for that!" The clerk advanced on them.

"Just hold on. I'll pay for it."

"Tucker!" Zoe persisted, shifting Nash to her other hip. "You have to read that…that trash. It's…none of it's true!"

The clerk's eyebrows rose, her gaze bouncing between Tucker and Zoe. "Oh em gee!" The girl squealed. "Will y'all sign a copy for me?"

Several people stopped to gawk. Tucker herded the women back inside the convenience store and found a spot where he could read the headlines. "Billionaire's Baby Mama Lives in Secret Love Nest. Barron Entertainment's second in command, Tucker Tate, hides his lover and their child on a private estate in Nashville." He pinched his nose and kept reading. It got worse. He backtracked to check the byline. Parker Grace. Of course. Had to be her. After the stunts the reporter pulled on his cousin, Senator Clay Barron, and Clay's wife Georgie, the woman was fired. He'd heard she was freelancing for whoever would buy a story.

His phone buzzed in his pocket. Pulling it out, he saw *Mom* flashing on the screen. He hit Ignore. Thirty seconds later, the screen flashed *Bridger*. He hit Ignore. For the next few minutes, his phone periodically pinged with calls from Chance Barron, his cousin and the family attorney, and Chance's brother Cash, who was Bridger's boss at Barron Security Services. He waited. It was just a matter of time before Chase, his own boss, called. And bingo. There it was.

"What are we gonna do?" Zoe spat out, keeping her voice low.

Tucker rubbed the back of his neck. "We're going to pay for whatever you're buying, including this rag.

I'm going to make some calls." He lifted a shoulder in a shrug looking far more nonchalant than he felt. "This isn't a big deal, angel. My family deals with this stuff all the time." They did, but this mess hit too close to home for comfort and it all seemed too orchestrated. Was someone after Zoe? Or him? He most definitely had a conference call in his future.

"But that's a whole pack of lies," she insisted.

"Need I remind you that this is a tabloid? The people who matter don't believe this stuff." Yeah, of course they didn't. The headlines had nothing to do with his phone blowing up. Nope. Not at all. "C'mon, darlin'. We need to get on the road."

And he needed to get to the bottom of things. Zoe didn't deserve this kind of attention. He stifled his anger as he considered the idea that this was his fault. Maybe he shouldn't have gotten so personally involved. Doubt shadowed his thoughts as he got to work.

Zoe wanted to find a deep, dark cave to crawl into. The tabloids were still at it, paparazzi constantly hounded her and Tucker and they'd had to hire extra security. What hurt, though, were the insinuations that she was on this tour not because of her talent, but because she was with Tucker. She tried not to let it affect her, but it did. She'd been so wound up last night, she'd picked a fight with Tucker. He'd slept on the couch.

He kept assuring her that the PR folks and his cousin's law firm were on top of things but it dang sure didn't feel that way. Zoe was terrified the whole mess would affect her singing, and her chance at a career.

Tucker had grown distant since all the stories hit. Somebody had managed to dig up Nash's birth certificate, and she was sure glad she'd left off the father's name, though that just fueled more rumors.

She had this one last concert to perform—at the University of Tennessee in Knoxville. Once it was done, she could go back to Mr. Don's guesthouse and lick her wounds. Just her and Nash. If she had to move out of Nashville and work little clubs and stuff, so be it. She wasn't sure she was cut out for all this craziness.

Normally, once her sound check was completed, she'd walk back to her RV. Security wanted her to wait until the Sons of Nashville were done so they could all go back together, which she did. Now, she walked between Tucker and Deacon, with the band and security surrounding them. The men scowled at the reporters.

Tucker gave her hand a squeeze. "We'll get through this and then we'll head back to Nashville tonight right after the concert. Okay?"

She nodded, unable to answer as a swarm of reporters descended. A reporter shouted, "Zoe, Zoe! I have it on good authority that your baby's father is doing life in prison—that he killed a man for you, and you ran off, leaving him to face arrest and the trial alone."

Oh, that got her dander up, but before she could respond, there was a commotion at the back of the pack. She recognized Parker Grace, and when Etta and Norbert Smithee appeared beside the reporter, Zoe stopped breathing. *Oh, hell no!*

"That woman framed my baby boy so she could take off with my grandbaby," Etta yelled. "I got the papers right here, all signed and legal, that Redmond wants me to raise his son, not that witch."

Pandemonium erupted. Tucker rushed her toward the RVs, burly bodyguards clearing the way. She needed to grab Nash and run away. No way in hell would she let that woman touch her baby. She stumbled but Tucker grabbed her up and held her in a princess carry as he jogged toward the circle of motor coaches, trucks, trailers and the Volunteermobile, the classic Winnebago normally parked in the Easleys' driveway.

Don and Rosemary had driven it to Knoxville in a fit of nostalgia. Their kids had all attended UT and every fall Saturday there was a home football game, the Easleys were there tailgating in the Volunteermobile.

The whole group crowded into Deacon's coach, leaving the guards outside to protect them. Zoe immediately snatched Nash from the play crib and cuddled him close, tears streaming down her cheeks.

"They're not gonna get you, baby boy. You hear me? Momma won't let those nasty people have you," she vowed into his sweet-smelling baby hair.

Deacon explained the situation while Tucker, his back to the group, made phone calls. Quin stood off to one side, watching Zoe, assessing her, as if Quin didn't quite trust her or this turn of events. *This isn't my fault!* Zoe wanted to scream. She didn't. She clamped her mouth shut and held on to Nash for all she was worth. She had to make a plan.

Zoe paced the length of the corridor that led to the stage. She did not want to be here, and her insides were so knotted up, breathing was painful. How was she going to sing? But how could she not? If she flaked out, her career would be as good as dead. If she ducked and ran, the paparazzi and the Smithees would still hound her, no matter where she went. Her daddy might not have been the best father in the world, but he'd taught her to keep her chin high, to stand up for herself and to not back down—not from anyone.

She was beginning to have a career. She had a bank account with money in it—money to take care of Nash. It all depended on her walking out on that stage, singing her heart out and fulfilling her contract. So that's just what she was gonna do. She had to get through tonight and then figure out all the rest. Like Tucker. If he didn't walk away from her after this. *No.* She couldn't think about him. She had songs to sing.

The stage manager whistled at her and she walked toward him, her gait determined. She was gonna rock the house—well, football stadium. She would raise her voice to the sky and give it all she had. And then she'd figure out what to do.

The stage manager walked her to her spot on the blacked-out stage and when the spotlight hit her, she was ready. She opened up with Miranda Lambert's "Gunpowder and Lead," a song that fit her mood perfectly. She'd show the Smithees—and everyone else—just what she was made of. She followed Miranda with "Redneck Woman," another anthem to strong women everywhere. The stadium was rocking. She slowed the tempo down with "Fancy," a song about a woman rising from dirt poor to rich man's wife. That only happened in songs and the movies, right?

When she finally got to the last song, she let the lights come down, waiting for the crowd to quiet just a bit—and for the Sons of Nashville to get into place behind her on the darkened stage. It felt like the whole place was holding its breath. Her fingers danced over the strings of her guitar as she slowly plucked the opening notes to "Rocky Top," the unofficial fight song of the University of Tennessee. Then, a cappella, she sang the first two lines of the chorus. Right on time, Xander, the Sons of Nashville's banjo picker, kicked in, upping the tempo. The audience erupted. Lights blazed on the stage and Deacon came out to join her as everyone sang.

The crowd was on their feet screaming by the time they were done. The audience's energy wrapped around her. Dang it. She *wanted* this. She deserved this and those damn Smithees wanted to take it all away. Her eyes burned with unshed tears when she took her bows and slipped offstage as Deacon and the Sons launched into their opening song, "Red Dirt Cowgirl."

Tucker wasn't waiting for her as she exited. Her chest tightened. Something was wrong. She headed for the greenroom at a trot but passed by the door when she heard angry voices farther on. She peeked around a corner to find Tucker, two of the Barron bodyguards and several stadium security guards facing down the Smithees, a weaselly little man in a ratty suit, and a big guy with stringy hair, fingerless leather gloves and a bad attitude.

"You're the one who doesn't understand," Ratty Suit whined. "My associate and I are here to ensure that justice is done. We have papers to serve and a pickup order for Baby Boy Smithee."

This. Was. Bad. Zoe panicked. Retreating to the greenroom, she slipped inside. She found Keisha, Quin and both kids. Zoe put away her guitar with studied calm even though her brain was whirring like margaritas in a blender. That's when Don Easley walked into the room and came over to her.

"I'm gonna get you and Nash outta here, darlin'. Get 'im packed up."

Zoe didn't stop to think. She slung the diaper bag over her shoulder, scooped up Nash in his carrier and her guitar, and headed for the door as Don said, "I'm takin' Zoe out the back way while everybody's otherwise occupied." They were gone before Quin could respond.

Don led her to an exit far away from the confrontation. He pressed a keyring into her hand. "Take the Volunteermobile. Nobody will look for you in that. Got your phone?" She nodded. "I'll let you know when it's safe to come back."

Come back? Would that ever be possible? What would Tucker do when he discovered her gone? She figured he'd be relieved to be rid of her but her secret heart hoped he'd miss her. And could get over being mad, because this would pretty much send him over the edge.

"Coast is clear." Don shoved a wad of money into her pocket and pushed her out the door. As much as she wanted to run, she walked sedately to avoid attention. Sticking to the shadows, she made it to the Volunteermobile with no one noticing. She fumbled the keys trying to unlock the door, dropped them. Crouching to pick them up, she heard voices and froze.

Tucker stared at the so-called attorney representing the Smithees. He'd brought a process server cum bounty hunter but no official law enforcement, much to his relief. He figured not even Quin would go up against real law enforcement. Of course, he didn't believe for one second that any judge had signed an order transferring Nash's custody to these people. Baby Boy Smithee? Seriously? With no father listed on the birth certificate, a real judge would demand DNA proof.

"As I've told you, I am Ms. Parker's representative. If you have official court papers to serve, you can serve me."

"But we want Redmond's baby," Etta Smithee said.

"Do you have proof he's the father?"

The attorney waved a sheaf of papers at him. "It's all right here. Sworn testimony."

Tucker snatched the papers and leafed through them. They carried only the seal and signature of a notary public. No judge of any jurisdiction. The attorney continued to whine. "Redmond woulda married the girl if that unfortunate incident hadn't happened. We're workin' on his appeal, and he should be gettin' out anytime now. He wants his momma to raise his boy till he's freed."

"Tucker!"

He turned at that sharp call. Quin stood in the hallway leading to the greenroom and the look on her face sent cold chills racing down his spine. He walked to her without a word. At her urgent whisper, he pivoted to stare out the glass doors leading to the parking lot. He was just in time to see the lights on an orange Winnebago flare to life. He went from standing still to a dead run, hitting the exit doors so hard they both banged back against the windows beside them.

Sprinting full-out, he reached the parking lot exit with seconds to spare. He planted his body in the middle of the drive, hands fisted on his hips. Tires squealed, but the RV kept coming, closer and closer. He caught a glimpse of Zoe's horrified face as a horn blared "Rocky Top."

Sixteen

"I could have killed you!" Zoe shook so hard the driver's seat rattled.

"But you didn't." Tucker stood beside her and tried to get his heart rate under control. Noise filtered in from outside, and he looked out the window. "Move over, I'm driving."

Zoe followed the direction of his gaze. A horde of reporters and photographers surged toward them in a menacing wave. Leading the pack was the Smithees, their ambulance-chasing lawyer and the thuggish process server. She squeaked and surrendered her seat.

"Buckle up," Tucker directed as he slid in behind her. He put the Winnebago in gear and pulled out onto the street just as the thug banged on the back of the RV. They left him in a cloud of diesel smoke.

"That was close." Pulling onto Neyland Drive, Tucker plotted the best way out of town.

"Where are we going?" Zoe's eyes were fixed on the side mirror.

"No clue. You were the one running away. Where were you going, Zoe? What were you going to do when you got there?"

She buried her face in her hands, and a few minutes later, Tucker caught her muffled, "I don't know."

He didn't get a lot of satisfaction from that answer. Tuck debated whether to ask the question on the tip of his tongue. The logical businessman knew it would be a mistake, but the man? The man wanted to know. In a quiet tone, he voiced his fear. "Were you running away from me?"

Zoe took too long to answer, and her silence was deafening. Tucker did not like the way it made him feel—angry, tense and…hurt. Her reticence made him question his feelings. Maybe he needed time to get his head on straight. He'd get her and Nash safely away, then Dandy Don and Deacon could look after them. Bent Star and the music business? Not his forte, obviously. It was time for him to get back to his real work. Except the thought of leaving Zoe and Nash left a hollow spot deep inside.

Nash fussed and without speaking, Zoe heaved out of the passenger seat and walked to the back of the RV. Tucker's phone played the theme from *Cops*. Quin. He swiped the phone and put it to his ear. "Yeah?"

"Seriously, Tucker? That girl—"

"Woman, Quin. She's a woman. And a mother. And she's in trouble. I don't want or need a lecture."

Silence stretched for almost a full minute. "Fine." He could almost hear Quin's teeth grinding. "You left the legal papers behind. I scanned and emailed them to Chance. Katherine says you need to go home."

"To Las Vegas?" Except that wasn't really home.

"No, dummy. *Home.* Oklahoma. The ranch. She's mobilizing the troops."

Now it was Tucker's turn for silence while he mulled it over. Katherine Tate was a force of nature. And despite his reluctance to get the Bee Dubyas involved, he had no such compunctions about their husbands or his brothers. When he approached the intersection with US 129, he turned north. "Okay," he agreed. "As soon as I hit I-40, we're heading west." He glanced at his phone to get the time. "We should be there around noon. Will you…"

"Yes. I'll call your mother." He pictured Quin rolling her eyes.

Zoe called from behind him. "Where are we going?"

"We're making a run for the border."

Zoe slept through the four-car wreck, the construction zones where they came to a complete halt and woke up just after dawn when Tucker pulled off at a travel center. In clipped words, he filled her in on the delays while maneuvering the Volunteermobile to a gas pump. He was filling the tank when she stepped out, Nash in a baby chest pack. She adjusted the UT baseball cap she'd swiped from the Volunteermobile's closet. "I'm going inside. Want food?"

He glanced up. Tucker looked…tired. Of course he was tired. He'd been driving all night. She'd had a nap at least. He shook his head, saying nothing. Yeah, he was still upset with her.

The first thing that caught her attention as she pushed through the entrance was the rack of tabloid papers lining the checkout area. Ducking her head, she headed to the ladies' room. When she came out, a few people stared.

She pushed past them, her hand pressing Nash's face to her chest, her own face down and veiled by her hair and the cap bill. Hungry, Zoe had planned to grab some hot breakfast to go from the buffet. Too late for that now. Awareness rolled through the crowd of people in the convenience store like rain moving across a field. She slipped through the exit. Would this circus never end?

Tucker joined her in the RV a few minutes later, holding two to-go boxes and a tall coffee cup. She popped one open to find scrambled eggs, bacon and sausage patties. The second held biscuits and gravy. "Hungry?"

Tucker shook his head. "Nope. That's all for you. Eat up." He left her sitting at the dinette. Shoving bites of biscuits covered in cream gravy into her mouth, she watched him while he got them back on the road. He was always feeding her. Taking care of her. She wondered if he realized what he was doing.

She ate, then gave Nash a bottle. Once he was asleep,

she settled into the passenger seat beside Tucker. He drove with his right hand, left elbow resting on the window ledge. The silence wasn't exactly comfortable. She huffed out a breath, which stirred her bangs. "I'm so sorry about all this."

"Not your fault, Zoe. We'll be home in a couple of hours."

Zoe. Her name. Not an endearment. Yeah, she'd really put her foot in it. She needed to fix things. "Going there will make a difference?"

He wheezed out a laugh. "I *have* mentioned my family, right?" She nodded but didn't say anything. "One cousin is a US senator. One is a fancy-smancy attorney no one wants to mess with. One owns a huge security company. My brothers all work for the Barrons in one form or another. The Barrons are a big deal in Oklahoma, and that stuff rolls downhill on us Tates."

Zoe mulled that over. "Good lord. How many of you are there?"

"Six Barrons, seven Tates."

She blinked. "Um...sibling rivalry much?"

Tucker laughed. The sound made her tummy do cartwheels. So often, Tucker looked serious and acted so single-minded but when he laughed? He was the sexiest man she'd ever seen. Yup, she had it bad, and she needed to get things settled because she didn't know where this whole deal was going.

"Thank you," she said.

He glanced over. "For what?"

"For being here for Nash and me."

He shrugged, returning his attention to the road.

She settled back against the seat. She liked Tucker. A lot. Too much. He made her want things she couldn't have and she was pretty sure he didn't want to give. Except he was so sweet to her and Nash.

They rode in silence until Tucker pulled off I-40 and into the Cherokee Travel Plaza. He stopped at the pumps, stretched and yawned. "We're about three hours away. We can take a break here."

The miles of silence left her with plenty of time to think and she'd finally figured out what was broken. Maybe. Nervous, she gazed at him. "Tucker?"

He stopped and turned to look at her. "I'm sorry."

"Not your—"

"It *is* my fault but that's not what I'm apologizing for. I…" She had to inhale to settle her stomach. "I panicked. I was just…running. So, yeah. In a way, I guess I was running away from you. If it means anything, I'm glad you caught me."

His smile came slow but didn't quite reach his eyes. "Are you sure?"

"Positive." She ached to touch him but kept her hands in her lap.

"I'm going to grab coffee with an extra shot of espresso. You want a mocha?"

Nodding, she said, "Tucker, are we—"

He cut her off. "It's all good."

She hoped it was.

Three people stood on the front porch—two men who looked a lot like Tucker flanking a woman. They all wore jeans and boots. Zoe eyed the formidable woman with trepidation. No wonder a touch of awe entered their voices whenever Tucker, Deacon or Dillon spoke of their mother. Dark hair, attractive and very much in charge. Zoe clutched Nash a little tighter.

"Mom, this is Zoe." Tucker said it like Mrs. Tate would know exactly who she was. He handed the empty baby carrier to the nearest man saying, "Zoe, this is Cooper." Then he urged her toward the front entrance without giving her a chance to gape, because there was a *lot* to gape at. The house was huge.

"About time y'all got here. Bring that baby inside." The woman swept her with a cool, appraising gaze, then her eyes flicked to the Volunteermobile, and her lips might have twitched just a little. The movement was so quick, Zoe couldn't be positive. "Come in, come in."

Like ducklings, the brothers followed their mother into the house. Zoe slipped through the door behind Tucker and followed the herd into an airy kitchen and family room.

"You're staying the night." Mrs. Tate said the words to Tucker but she was staring at Zoe. "I have your room ready, Tucker."

Tucker leaned down only a little bit to kiss his mother on the cheek. "Thanks, Mom."

"And we're having fried chicken and all the fixings for lunch," Mrs. Tate said, giving Zoe another long look. A thought hit her. What would happen if Katherine Tate tangled with Etta Smithee? A scene of the two women wrestling in a WWE ring popped into her head and Zoe burst out laughing.

"Zoe can stay, too."

Yippee, Zoe thought, a touch apprehensive.

"But she sleeps in the guest room."

Well, that was a no-brainer. Zoe shifted Nash to her other hip. His mother watched.

"Zoe, stay. The rest of you, out of here."

The woman shooed her sons out of the kitchen like they were chickens. Not one lingered.

"Sit, girl," Mrs. Tate ordered.

What was she, a dog? Sit. Stay. But who was she to argue? Zoe hitched her hip on a tall stool at the kitchen island. "I'll be happy to help cook, ma'am."

"You can help by telling me what's going on between you and my son."

She gulped. That was a good question—one she'd like the answer to herself. "Not quite sure what you mean, Miz Tate."

"Call me Katherine. And don't play dumb, Zoe. You aren't. You know exactly what I mean. You and my son are sleeping together, and don't think for a minute that he won't try to sneak into your room tonight."

Zoe blushed and fussed with Nash's clothing for a moment to regain her equilibrium. Katherine kept right on talking.

"My sons are grown men, Zoe, and they aren't saints. Their father and I prepared them for the real world as best we could and raised them to be responsible, caring men. Now that Deacon has settled down—given he was the wildest in the bunch—I have hopes for the rest of them. I want to know about you."

Shoulders square, chin jutting, Zoe faced down the

older woman. "Since your daughter-in-law ran a background check on me, I figure you pretty much know everything there is to know."

"My son Bridger checked long before Quin even thought of it." She poured a glass of sweet tea and slid it over the countertop to Zoe. "Don't get your panties in a twist. That's the way this family works. Always has. We like to know who we're dealing with. You notice that you are still part of Tucker's life, yes?"

Zoe closed her mouth with a snap and focused on her glass of tea. "What's that mean?"

"It means that I trust my sons. And it means that Tucker cares about you. There is no way he'd be caught dead driving a Tennessee-orange Winnebago with the UT emblem plastered on the back otherwise. That boy's a graduate of the University of Oklahoma and his blood runs crimson and cream."

Zoe snickered, and took a drink to help disguise her amusement. "Yeah. He's had to toot the horn a time or two. I thought he was gonna go apoplectic or something."

Katherine knitted her brow. "Don't tell me it plays 'Rocky Top.'" Zoe nodded and Mrs. Tate burst out laughing. She was about to take a sip of her drink when a new man walked in. He had to be another Tate brother. He was older, with crinkles at the corners of his eyes and a watchful air about him.

"Hunter, this is Zoe Parker. And Nash." Katherine sidled over and plucked Nash out of her lap before Zoe could react. "Here," the woman said, passing the baby to him. "You need practice. Now get out of here until lunchtime." She fluttered her hands at him, moving him along.

"Hey!" Zoe protested.

He scowled but did as his mother asked, though he glanced over his shoulder. "Nice to meet you, Zoe. Don't worry, I'll take Nash to Tucker."

Katherine poured her own glass of tea and settled on a stool across from Zoe. She took several sips, then sighed and said, "You've got my son worried, Zoe."

"Which one?"

The look Tucker's mother leveled on her would have turned a steel magnolia into a puddle of goo. "Do not play dumb with me, young lady."

Zoe blinked and leaned away from the intensity in Katherine's stare. "What would Tucker be worried about?"

"You. And your baby. Tucker has feelings for you. Deep ones. I want to know if you return them. If not, tell him now and put him out of his misery."

She hung her head. Zoe did have feelings but admitting them? It left her too vulnerable. "I'll talk to him."

Seventeen

Tucker watched Zoe and his mother from his hiding place like they were players in a tennis match. He'd thought to hang back to hear their discussion but then Hunter walked down the hall where he was eavesdropping. His big brother handed the kid off and pushed him on down the hallway.

"Mom catches you, there'll be trouble. Besides, we need to talk."

That didn't bode well. Neither did Cooper and Bridger standing in the game room like gate sentries. With their feet spread and arms crossed over their chests, they radiated determination. "You're the last one of us I'd pick to be in this mess," Bridger said. Hunter and Cooper agreed.

"I know what I'm doing." Tucker glowered at his brothers.

"We don't think you do." This from Cooper.

The *intervention* went downhill from there. Oddly, Hunter never said a word and Tucker wondered whose side his big brother was on. Nash finally saved him with a dirty diaper. His mom called them in for lunch as he finished changing the baby.

Zoe picked at her food. His brothers kept up a running commentary of their lives. Tucker shoveled food into his mouth. His mom was a great cook, and homemade fried chicken with mashed potatoes, gravy, biscuits and fresh green beans was his favorite meal. And with his mouth full of food, he didn't have room to stick his foot in there.

After nibbling on a drumstick and stirring gravy around in the mashed potatoes on her plate, Zoe slipped out of her chair and carried her plate into the kitchen. Tucker watched his mother watch Zoe. Then her gaze focused on him with laser-sharp accuracy. Of course, his three brothers also turned their gazes on him.

"Don't y'all work for a living?" he muttered.

"It's Sunday," Bridger reminded him.

"Hence, fried chicken for lunch?" Cooper hinted, like they hadn't had fried chicken for Sunday lunch their entire lives.

Tucker glared at Hunter, waiting for his oldest brother to weigh in, but Bridger spoke up instead. "Speaking of lunch, guess who I ran into the other day?" he said to Hunter, who looked bored and took another bite. "Tanya McDaniels."

Hunter choked as the rest of them froze, all eyes on Bridger. "Seems she's moved back to Oklahoma City."

Gulping the iced tea in his glass, Hunter seemed to have his breathing back under control, though his temper wasn't. "In case you've forgotten, Bridger, that's not a name I want repeated. We clear on that?" Hunter pushed back from the table, his chair scraping on the wooden floor. He cleared his plate and followed Zoe to the kitchen.

Silence reigned for several long moments, then Katherine rose and walked out of the room. Cooper hit Bridger in the biceps. Hard. "Way to go, numbnuts."

"I thought he needed to know." Bridger shrugged. "That whole deal with Tanya was screwed up, even to me, and I was just a kid. We all know she messed him over while he was deployed with the Marines." He muttered a few strong words under his breath, none of them flattering. "Just sayin'."

Tucker scraped the last bit of gravy off his plate with his biscuit, stuffed it into his mouth and stood. He smacked the back of Bridger's head with his palm, gathered his plate and headed to the kitchen before his brother could retaliate. He glanced out the French doors and saw his mother and Hunter sitting on the back porch talking. Nash was secured in his carrier on the kitchen island, playing grabby-toes and giggling. Zoe was washing dishes.

"You don't have to do that, angel."

"Yeah I do." Though quiet, Zoe's voice was filled with conviction. "Gotta pay my own way, and with the Smithees—"

"C'mere." Tucker cut her off and pulled her into his arms. He kissed the top of her head, speaking into her hair. "Let me explain something about my family. We stick together. When one of us is in trouble, we all come running to help. That includes our cousins, the Barrons. It'll be all right, Zoe. I promise."

Zoe stiffened. "Don't make promises you can't keep. The Smithees have that awful lawyer workin' for 'em. They're gonna make a big ol' stink and I've dragged your family right into the middle of it."

"My family wants—"

Nash wailed, cutting him off. Zoe ducked around Tucker, snagged the carrier and swung it off the island. She then grabbed a bottle from the refrigerator. "I gotta feed Bugtussle."

Tucker wanted to follow her to explain that *he'd* involved his family and why, but the appearance of his cousin, Chance, a drumstick in one hand and a folder in the other, had him reversing directions. "The study," he directed. By the time they arrived in the cozy den-like space his father once used as an office, Chance had finished the chicken. Tucker settled a hip on one corner of the desk while Chance stood in front.

"I emailed Zoe's recording contract to Don Easley," Chance said without preamble. "Now, I just have one question for you, Tuck." Tucker raised both brows in a look of inquiry, waiting for him to continue. "I've talked to Redmond Smithee. How much money are you willing to pay him to sign away his parental rights?" He stopped Tucker from answering with another question. "Why are you doing this, cuz?"

Good question. He dropped his chin and rubbed the back of his neck. "Already had the familial intervention, *cuz*."

"No intervention, Tucker. I just want you to think things through. So, back to my original questions. How much and why?"

How much was easy. Why? He wasn't impetuous. He didn't just *do* crazy stuff like pick up a runaway bride stranded on the side of the road. He didn't help babies get born. He didn't fall for sweet-voiced country girls. Except he'd done all those things. He'd probably been falling in love with Zoe since the moment he stuffed that awful wedding dress around her in his T-Bird.

"I've got another question, Tuck. Have you talked to Zoe about this? About terminating the father's parental rights?"

That question he could easily answer. He squarely met Chance's gaze. "No, but she didn't list Smithee on the birth certificate. A DNA test would prove he's the father so I want that preempted. She wants those people out of her life, and out of her son's." Tucker breathed. "As for your other questions, first, how much? However much it takes." He'd pay a million dollars to get the Smithees out of Zoe's and Nash's lives. Hell, he'd pay ten million.

"As for the why?" He looked down at the toes of his boots before answering. "Because I'm fairly certain I'm falling in love."

"That's all I needed to know." Chance spread out the papers from the file on the desk. "I need a cashier's check for one hundred thousand dollars. I'll fly to Alabama tomorrow with the check, get Smithee to sign the papers and then I'll put those funds in a trust account for him and his family. Now sign here, here and here."

As Tucker signed, he said quietly, "How big a deal would adoption papers be?"

"A bit premature, don't you think?" Chance looked concerned. "Given the circumstances?"

Tucker lifted one shoulder in a studied shrug. "Yeah, maybe. But you know me. I'm a planner. Just in case, I want them ready. For when the time comes."

Chance favored him with a searching look, as he gathered the papers. "If that's what you want, bud." It sounded like a question.

The two of them headed for the back door. Katherine was puttering around in the kitchen, Zoe nowhere in sight. Chance paused to kiss his aunt on the cheek and then, with her admonition to toss the drumstick in the trash on his way out, he laughed and did. Tucker breathed easy for the first time in a while. Getting the Smithees out of Zoe's life was worth every penny.

"That's a lot of money," his mother said in a soft voice—one he knew far too well. She was not happy.

"It's my money, Mom. And you shouldn't have been eavesdropping."

"This is my house, and you're my son. I'll do whatever it takes to protect both. What do you really know about this girl, Tucker?"

"I know everything I need to."

"Is she worth a hundred thousand dollars?" Katherine held up her hand. "Think about it before you answer me. Examine your motives, son. Chase is married now. And Deacon, who stumbled into a ready-made family. You always did try to imitate both of them."

He bristled. "That's not what I'm doing, Mom."

"It's okay to care about this girl and her baby, but do you really need to get so involved? She might be talented—and according to Deacon and Dillon, she is. But how long would it take her to pay you back?"

"I don't want her to pay me back."

"I don't understand you, Tucker."

"I don't exactly understand you at the moment, Mom. I thought you liked Zoe."

"I do. But she's not the woman for you." His mother wiped her hands on a dish towel hung on the horseshoe nailed to the cabinet over the sink. "She has a child, Tucker. A child who isn't yours. You're an executive with a Fortune 100 company. She's…she wants to be an entertainer. How will that work? She won't be home to take care of her child or you. Or do you plan to trail around after her like a well-trained dog?"

"That's enough, Mom. We're done here."

"We're not even close. Who gives up their dream, Tucker? Have you thought about that? Your life is in Las Vegas or wherever else Barron Entertainment needs you. That apartment at the Crown Casino is as close to a home as you have when you aren't here. In the room you grew up in. You stay in condos owned by the company when you travel. You need a real home. A real wife. Suppose it does work out between the two of you. Will you stay in Vegas while she lives in Nashville? Do you live separate lives with a nanny looking after her baby? Or do you give up everything you've worked for just so she can do what she wants?"

He growled under his breath, unwilling to admit he hadn't thought things through completely, which was so unlike him. He was the logical one, the one who made plans and followed them. Or he had been until he met Zoe. Ever since he'd picked her up on the side of the road, he'd been running on emotional adrenaline. Maybe he did need to step back and assess the situation. Except he didn't have to. He knew how he felt.

Zoe and Nash…he loved them.

Tucker, jostling Nash against his shoulder, watched Zoe slap icing on a blue cake. The thing looked like half a ball. The icing was white and there was a package of coconut flakes on the counter. Maybe it was supposed to look like a snowball.

"Ah, darlin'?"

"What?" She glanced up and he saw a dab of icing on her cheek. He had to refrain from licking it off.

"What are you doing?"

"What does it look like I'm doing? I baked a cake and now I'm icing it."

"Fair enough. *Why* did you bake a cake?"

"Because…well… I needed something to do. I've been here three days." She tore the bag of coconut open with her teeth and began throwing handfuls at the cake. She finally stopped, then backed away until her butt was braced against the stainless steel Sub-Zero refrigerator. Shoving her hands into her pockets, which caused her shoulders to curve forward in a dejected slump, she huffed out a breath. "You just don't get it."

Something in her voice kept him silent when he would have offered up a quip or worse, some meaningless platitude. Tucker waited. He seemed to be doing a lot of that lately.

"I want to be a singer, Tucker," she said, almost in a whisper. He had to strain to understand her words.

"You *are* a singer, Zoe. What does this have to do with baking a cake?"

In a stronger voice, though one thick with tears, she added, "Nothin'. I just… It's…it was somethin' nice to do for your family."

His instincts told him to gather her into his arms. When he walked toward her, she held up her hands to halt him. "My whole life, all I've ever wanted to be is a singer. I want the albums and the studio time and performing in an arena in front of thousands of fans. I wanna win Entertainer of the Year from the Country Music Association."

He didn't catch the smile forming on his mouth in time. Her lips thinned but not in anger. Too late, Tucker realized her bottom lip was trembling.

"Your family feels sorry for me. I know people take one look at me and think I'm a joke. Just some no-account hillbilly girl with stars in her eyes." Her gaze flicked to the baby in his arms. "One too dumb not to get pregnant by a stranger and then not smart enough to take care of it if her career is that all-fired important."

He tried to interrupt her. "That's not true, Zoe."

"I might be from the back of beyond, but so was

Miss Dolly. So were a lot of country stars before they came to Nashville and made a name for themselves. I can sing. I'm not afraid to work hard, and I'll do whatever it takes to make my dream come true and take care of my baby boy." Her head *thunked* against the metal fridge. "Well…not exactly *whatever.* I'll get there on my talent, not my back."

That got his attention—not that she didn't have it before. "Zoe—"

"No. Hear me out. I don't wanna believe that you think I'm doin' the deed with you to get a contract with Bent Star, but I gotta wonder." Her gaze was steady as she looked at him. "I got dreams. Big ones. Important ones. Important to me, anyway. I always have. And nobody is gonna stop me."

"I'm not trying to stop you, Zoe. In fact—" He was about to tell her that Dandy Don had her contract from Bent Star, that he wanted to sign her and not because he'd mixed business with pleasure but because he believed in her, but he didn't get the chance.

Because just then, Bridger walked in, a tabloid rolled up in one hand and a business card in the other. He paused, staring at Zoe, his face inscrutable. Tucker straightened as Bridge tossed the items onto the island.

"Bridge?" Tucker stared at his brother, concerned.

"Found this stuff in Nash's diaper bag when I changed him earlier."

Tucker recognized the tabloid—and its secret love nest headline. He picked up the card and he clenched his teeth when he read the name. "Parker Grace?"

Tucker tore his eyes from his brother and focused

on Zoe. “What is this? Have you had contact with this woman?” Zoe’s voice rang in his head. *I’ll do whatever it takes to make my dream come true.* Had he been so wrong about Zoe? Had she been working with the one reporter his whole family hated?

To say the mood in the room was tense was an understatement. “She ambushed me at Dandy Don’s. I told her to leave. You can check. I called nine-one-one to report it.” Zoe’s gaze darted between the two men, as she worried they didn’t believe her. Her heart broke a little and then her temper flared. “Why in the deep, dark recesses of hell would I want my name splashed all over the tabloids?”

“Publicity,” Bridger said.

“Seriously? Y’all are crazy. Bein’ tabloid trash sucks. Y’all don’t know what it’s like havin’ people stare at you like you’re cow manure stuck on the bottom of their boots.”

“Zoe. We’ve never… *I’ve* never—”

She marched up to Tucker, plucked Nash from his arms and cuddled the baby close. She stared at the men—there was no compassion in Bridger’s eyes and only confusion in Tucker’s. Hot tears pricked the back of her eyelids. She would not cry. She would not show them how much this hurt. She should have expected something like this to happen. Bad stuff always did and she’d been a damn fool for ever thinking that she and Tucker might have something real and lasting. She was just a girl from the wrong side of the tracks who could sing a little and he was Tucker Tate, Mr. Billionaire Country, or he would be if there was a beauty contest like that.

She had to reach deep for some dignity and deeper still to find the stubbornness that saw her through every bad thing that happened in her life. She didn't need Tucker Tate. Didn't want him. Much. But she'd just learned something, and sometimes the lessons of the heart were the hardest and most painful. If he didn't trust her, he'd never care about her.

"Zoe."

Tucker reached for her but she dodged him. "I'm done here."

Zoe stomped out of the kitchen, flying on adrenaline. She couldn't stay in the same room with Tucker. Heck, she couldn't stay in the same house with him. She'd pack up her and Nash's stuff and go stay in the RV.

While she gathered their belongings, she came up with a plan. Digging out her cell, she called Dandy Don. She swallowed hard, forcing her voice to stay firm but failing as she said, "Hi, Mr. Don."

"Are you okay, darlin'?" His voice, while full of fatherly concern, sounded far away.

"Yeah. I'm fine." She could lie now because she would be fine. Eventually. "I wanted to let you know I'm headin' back to Nashville to return your Volunteermobile. I'll be there tomorrow."

"Is Tucker—"

"No." She cut him off. "He ain't. I'm drivin' back alone." It wasn't like Tucker and his family wanted her there.

"I'm not sure that's a good—"

"We'll be fine, Mr. Don, Nash and me." And they would be because she was taking back her life.

Eighteen

Tucker stared into his coffee cup, the reflection staring back at him looking morose. The call from Don Easley that morning had been a double whammy—Zoe was driving back to Nashville and Midnight Records had offered her a contract. Dandy Don refused to discuss the terms, which made Tuck suspicious, given how liberal Bent Star's contract was.

As Bridger and his mother entered the kitchen, he snarled. "She's gone." He ignored the look they exchanged.

"We know," Bridger said, pouring his own cup. "I called in a favor from a federal agent who owed me one. He did some checking. It was those Smithee people stirring up the press. And we all know Parker Grace has a grudge against us." He pulled a stool up next to Tucker and clapped his shoulder. "I'm sorry. I was wrong about Zoe."

"Me, too," Quin added as she and Deke walked in, followed by the rest of his family.

"It doesn't matter." How could he have been so totally…stupid? There was a reason he didn't do relationships. And now he'd pretty much ruined whatever chance he had with Zoe—personally *or* professionally. Deke had been right to warn him. He felt hollow inside.

"I'm disappointed in you, Tucker."

That brought his head up, and he was too stunned to avoid scowling at his mother. "Excuse me? You're the one who insisted she'd never be a real wife, that she wasn't good enough for me."

"And you're the one who was supposed to fight for her if you loved her."

Tucker opened and closed his mouth several times, unable to form coherent words. Reverse psychology? *That* was his mother's plan? Deke shooed everyone out, a gesture Tucker appreciated. He didn't need—or want—his brothers to see his misery. Their mother remained in the doorway, lips pursed, eyes fixed on him. He'd messed up. Bad. And while Katherine Tate loved her sons, she never hesitated to call them on the carpet when they were wrong. Tucker buried his face in his hands, unable to meet the censure in his mother's gaze any longer.

He glanced up, hoping to be alone, but Deke had remained, though his mother was gone. Silence stretched between him and his older brother. Tucker waited for Deke to break it. Deke didn't.

"Go ahead," Tucker finally said. "I know you're dying to tell me what an idiot I am."

"Naw. It'd be too much like kicking a puppy."

Tucker raised his head, stared at his brother. "I didn't get it."

"Dude, you're a guy. Most of us don't until some smart woman nails us with a clue-by-four." Deke hitched a hip on a stool and folded his arms across his chest. "The question becomes, what are you going to do about it?"

"She has an offer from Midnight Records. If she signs with—" Tucker bit his tongue when his brother reached over and cuffed the back of his head. "Owww."

"This isn't about Zoe signing with another label. This is about your feelings for her, and hers for you."

"Yeah, but…" Tucker huffed out a breath and scrubbed at his hair. Feelings. He didn't want to talk about *feelings* with his brother.

"You need to talk to her."

"I tried calling. She wouldn't pick up."

"Then go after her."

"She has a head start."

Deke rolled his eyes. "How are we even related? Tuck, who do you work for?"

"Barron Entertainment."

"And what is your title?"

"Chief Operations Officer."

"And what's sitting in a hangar at Wiley Post Airport?"

Tuck stared at Deke and scrunched his forehead,

thinking hard. He brought up his hands and lifted his shoulders in a gesture that said, *What?*

Deke sighed dramatically then said each word slowly. "The corporate jets, including the one we all flew in on last night."

He leaned forward until his forehead bounced a little on the granite counter. "Brain-dead. I'm totally brain-dead." He'd been so wrapped up in misery that his calm, collected and highly organized mind simply shorted out.

But now hope loosened the knot in his chest. He could be in Nashville before Zoe got there. He could meet her before she did something they'd both regret. He could fix this. All he had to do was grovel. He could learn to do that in the two hours it would take to fly there. And he would. Grovel. Until he got her back.

"You also need to make a grand gesture."

"A what?"

"A grand gesture. To show her how much she means to you."

"Like what?"

"Like Chance telling Uncle Cyrus to take a flying leap and helping Cassie with that cattle drive."

That had been a grand gesture. Their Uncle Cyrus had been a tyrant trying to ruin Cassie's life. To meet a payment on a bank loan, and with no other way to get her herd to market, Cassie pulled off—with Chance's help—a modern-day cattle drive.

Deke's smile softened. "Like Quin standing in front of the stage on New Year's Eve holding up a sign asking me for a second chance." Tucker stared at Deke, his mind blank. “Seriously? I really am starting to doubt we’re related. Do you remember how furious I was over losing Noelle?” Tucker nodded. “I know I told you how she apologized in front of the whole crowd.”

“So?”

“So? You’re hopeless. Go pack. I’ll call the hangar. Maybe you’ll think of something before you get to Nashville.”

Zoe paced the backstage area of the Grand Ole Opry. Two days after returning to Nashville, Mr. Don called to say she was appearing at the Opry on Saturday night. It was almost time. She’d rehearsed two songs with the Opry’s back-up musicians: Gretchen Wilson’s “Redneck Woman” and Striking Matches’ “When the Right One Comes Along.” Mr. Don was convinced they’d showcase her voice perfectly, even though the second song was a duet. The last time she’d sung it had been at Bent Star. Given her situation with Tucker, the lyrics ripped her heart open. Her stomach knotted, and she wanted to throw up but there wasn’t time. The announcer was introducing her.

“You got this, darlin’,” Mr. Don said, giving her a pat on the shoulder. “Now get out there and show ’em what you got.”

She plastered on a big smile she didn’t feel and strode into the spotlight like she’d been born for this moment. The show always went on.

The crowd loved the first song, clapping and shouting along with her. When she launched into the second song, a hush fell over the audience and when the chorus arrived, she sensed their anticipation. Surprised almost speechless, she just managed not to drop a note when Deacon appeared beside her to sing the duet. This shouldn't be happening since she'd left Tucker—and Bent Star.

As the last sad notes echoed in the auditorium, the crowd went wild. She took her bows and accepted a kiss on the cheek from Deacon. She turned to leave the stage, but Deke snagged her arm and hauled her back to the microphone.

"As y'all know, Zoe's been opening for the Sons of Nashville the past couple of weeks," Deke said into the mic. "Not only is she a fantastic performer, she's a heckuva songwriter, too." The crowd whistled. "Zoe doesn't know what I'm about to say and I'm hopin' she won't be mad."

Confused, Zoe stared at Deacon and mouthed, "What are you talking about?"

He winked at her and continued. "Tonight, I'm pleased that the Sons and I get to back her up on the debut of her new song, 'We Can't Be.' Ladies and gentlemen, Zoe Parker!"

Zoe stopped breathing. Her first instinct was to run off the stage but before her panic won, Deke leaned close and whispered in her ear. "You got this, darlin', just like we practiced all those times in all those greenrooms. Yeah?"

The lights lowered, and the Sons played the opening bridge before Zoe was ready. They played it a second time before she gathered enough wits to join in on her guitar. Third time through was the charm and she opened her mouth to sing. “I’m not lookin’ for true love, ’cause I’ll just find a broken heart. But when I look at you, I want to give you everything.”

The band joined in with backup vocals on the chorus. “You can’t be the hero, not in my story. You aren’t the kind of man who would ever share the glory. You won’t ever love me. We just can’t be.”

The second verse was just her and her guitar. “You can’t be the one for me, no matter how hard I wish it. But when you look at me, I want to give you everything.” Her plaintive voice filled every corner of the Grand Ole Opry. The band sang the chorus while she remained silent.

When she belted out the third verse and final chorus, the music rose to a crescendo. “You’re standin’ there watchin’ me through eyes that are full of lies. But when you turn to leave, I want to give you everything. I still want to give you everything, but you won’t ever be the hero, not in my story. You aren’t the kind of man who would ever share the glory. You won’t ever love me, we just can’t be. We can’t be.”

Tucker waited in the wings, a huge bouquet of roses and fancy flowers he couldn’t name. He also had a small velvet box tucked in the pocket of his jacket. He was as ready as he’d ever be. He was also so nervous he couldn’t stand still. Shifting from foot to foot, he breathed deep through the tangle of nerves tying him into knots. This was his moment to fix everything. This would work. It had to. And he owed Deacon and Dillon big-time. His brothers had really come through for him—and for Zoe. Deke worked his magic and contacts with the Opry, and Dillon had been the one to help Zoe refine the song while they toured.

He could see part of the audience but mostly, he focused on Zoe. Hearing her sing, listening to the crowd's reaction, seeing the surprise on her face when Deke joined her, then the Sons performing *her* song… Once she came off the stage he'd show her how much he loved her.

The words Zoe sang hit him. Hard. He realized he'd never heard this song all the way through. "You're standing there watchin' me through eyes that are full of lies." Did she think he'd lied to her? Was he too late? Surely not. Surely, she would let him explain. Let him tell her how he felt. About her. About Nash. But the words hit home, as sharp as an ice pick jamming into his heart.

The song ended, and she got a standing ovation—just like she deserved. For the first time in his life, he was panicked at the thought of talking to a woman. No, not *a* woman. *This* woman. The woman who owned his heart, the woman he wanted to spend the rest of his life with. She came off the stage surrounded by Deke and the band, and then Dandy Don was there, steering her toward a group of men. People swarmed the backstage area as they set up for the next entertainer, and he lost sight of Zoe for a moment. He finally spotted her in the hallway leading to the dressing rooms. He walked up as Easley introduced the men.

"Zoe, I'd like you to meet Chuck Goodman, Dan

Decker, Bill Albright and Joe Henderson from Midnight Records."

Zoe's smile lit up every dingy backstage corner until she caught sight of him. Her expression blanked before she turned away. The men crowded around her, touching and complimenting, and Tucker's vision narrowed to red-and-green flashes of anger and jealousy.

The Midnight Records deal should have been dead. No way Don would let Zoe sign with them. Or would he? Tucker pushed forward again, his hand raised to catch her attention. Then he heard words that sliced through his heart like a razor.

"Your performance tonight was a test you passed with flying colors. Let's talk about your recording contract."

"Thank y'all so much for doing this!" The excitement in Zoe's voice was another slash. "Let's go to my dressing room and talk."

He just stood there as they walked away. Zoe ignored him. When a stagehand jostled him, Tucker gathered up what little dignity he had left, turned and headed for the exit. An industrial-sized trashcan flanked the door.

"Tucker! Hey, Tucker! Wait up!"

He glanced over his shoulder to see Deacon dodging around people trying to catch up with him. Staring pointedly at his brother, Tucker lifted the lid of the trashcan and dumped the bouquet, along with the card he'd written, inside.

So much for grand gestures and falling in love.

Nineteen

Zoe stared at the contract. All she had to do was sign her name and every dream she'd ever hoped for would come true. A recording contract. An album. Her own tour. Well, eventually. They promised she'd be a headliner before a year was out. After all, they were the ones who'd arranged for her to appear at the Opry, according to Bill Albright, Midnight Records' promotions manager. They'd hinted that Deke and the Sons agreed to perform with her because Midnight was looking to acquire Bent Star. She should be excited about their interest. Yeah. *Should be* was the operative phrase.

"You don't have to sign it tonight," Dandy Don said, quietly shutting the door behind him.

She glanced up and saw the huge bouquet of roses

and other blooms he was holding. “Aw, Mr. Don, you didn’t need to—”

“I didn’t,” he quickly interjected.

Zoe was confused. “Then who did?”

“An admirer. If you’re ready, I’ll drive you home.”

She gathered up the contract and stuffed it into her guitar case. Grabbing her belongings, she followed him out of the dressing room.

“Don’t forget your flowers, Zoe,” Don reminded. The parking lot was mostly empty but lights shone everywhere. *I’m country roads and he’s straight-up city lights.* Someday, she’d write that song when thoughts of Tucker didn’t hurt so much.

By the time they’d pulled up at the guesthouse, Zoe had made her decision. She turned to Don. “Do I sign it and give it to you?”

“Sign what, darlin’?”

“The contract.”

“Which one?”

Startled, she blinked at him. “What do you mean which one?”

“There’s another offer on the table.”

“You didn’t tell me that!”

He reached over and patted her shoulder. “I didn’t mean for you to decide tonight, sugar. The boys from Midnight were insistent about seeing you and presenting their contract. Their biggest backer is gettin’ pushy. We’ll talk tomorrow. You’ve had a big night. Go get some sleep.”

Zoe grabbed her things, including the bouquet, from the back seat and headed inside. Rosemary Easley, who'd been babysitting, met her at the door, gave her a hug, then joined her husband. Zoe stood at the threshold, watching until they were out of sight. Finding a plastic pitcher under the sink, she filled it with water and stuffed the flowers into it. They smelled sweet. An admirer, Mr. Don had said. Maybe Deke and the boys in the band.

Two contracts. Singing at the Opry. Her thoughts kept zinging around her brain like a pinball on steroids, but she crawled into bed and tried to sleep.

Nash was up early, as usual. Zoe wondered how people worked nights and dealt with kids on a daytime schedule. She dragged herself into the kitchen, warmed a bottle and fixed coffee. Good thing she could yawn and feed Nash at the same time. Her eyes kept straying to the flowers. Who'd sent them to her? If not the Sons, maybe it was the men from Midnight.

Two cups of coffee later, she noticed a card tucked into the ribbons and greenery. Curious, she pulled it out. Three words caught her attention.

Deacon walked through the front door of the town house without knocking. Tucker glowered at his brother. "Go away, Deke."

"What happened? I saw you dump the flowers."

"Nothing. Obviously."

Tucker wasn't in the mood for brotherly concern.

"Are you sulking?" Deke asked, dropping into one of the guest chairs.

"No." He wasn't. Sulking didn't even come close to what he was feeling.

"Look, Tuck. Zoe will get over her snit and—"

"Snit? Did you hear that song, Deacon? I mean you *were* singing the damn thing with her."

Deacon held his hands out in a soothing gesture. "Easy, little brother. It's just a song."

"About me." Tucker challenged Deke with a look. "You know it is." His brother shrugged but didn't dispute his assertion. Tucker buried his face in his hands and mumbled, "I royally screwed up everything."

"Wow. Pity party much?"

Raising his head, he glowered at Deke. He was entitled because…well, because. "And so much for your grand gestures. She thinks Midnight Records got her the Opry gig."

"Why would she think that?"

"How the hell should I know, but she thanked them for it last night right before she ushered them into her dressing room to talk about their contract."

"Was Don there?"

"Yeah."

Deke rubbed his chin between thumb and forefinger, thinking. "He would have set her straight. And discussed the contract Bent Star offered." He leaned forward. "What I don't get is why you didn't barge in there, run them off and make your case."

Tucker's scowl turned into disbelief. "I ask again, did you hear the words to her song?"

"Seriously, dude. You need to get over yourself. She was writing that song before you two broke up." Deke held up his hands to stay Tucker's retort. "I repeat. It's *just* a song, written by a talented songwriter.

She's writing a song for me and you aren't anywhere in the lyrics."

"So what's your point?" Tucker was still grumpy.

"Do you love the girl?"

"Of course I do."

"Is she worth fighting for?"

Tucker's answer was a dirty look with a side helping of derision.

"Then I rest my case. Why aren't you tracking her down and telling her how you feel?" Deacon studied him. Tucker ignored his brother.

"You're going to let Midnight Records steal your star *and* the love of your life? Since when did failure become an option for you, little bro?"

Traffic was backed up for blocks. Between a series of accidents and construction, the two lanes going his direction were at a complete standstill. After hearing that Zoe had an appointment there this afternoon, he was headed downtown to Midnight Records' office located in a high-rise building. Steel and glass. Cold. Impersonal. Just like Midnight Records. They wouldn't know what to do with a talented singer like Zoe. They'd use her up and toss her aside once they got their pound of flesh. Why would Don counsel her to sign with them? If he got there in time, he'd convince Zoe to...what? Sign with Bent Star? Marry him? Yes, that's exactly what he'd do.

With the window down on the SUV, he heard horns blare. Above them all came a sound that made him laugh—a horn that played "Rocky Top." He caught a glimpse of Don Easley's RV turning the corner. He followed it. He still had time, could still fix the fragile thing growing between them that he'd broken.

Failure is not an option. The words beat out a rhythm in his brain. He kept his eyes on the prize—the Volunteermobile. The vehicle was dead ahead. *Failure is not an option.* He chanted it over and over in his head. He looked around and realized he was headed back toward the town house. He caught up to the RV as it stopped in front of his house. He threw the transmission into Park and leaped out. Banging on the RV's door, he waited for it to open. When it did, Zoe stood there, staring down at him.

She crossed her arms over her chest in a protective gesture. "Tucker—"

He interrupted her. "Don't sign with Midnight Records."

"Why?"

"Because I love you."

Her face softened. "Yeah?" she whispered.

"I wanna be the hero in your story, Zoe."

"You do?"

"Always, angel. Will you let me?" He cupped her face, brushing away a tear with his thumb. "I never meant to hurt you, Zoe. And I do believe in you. Don has a contract for you from Bent Star." Zoe tried to speak, but Tucker continued talking over the top of her protests. "And *I* set up the gig last night at the Opry, with Deke and the band to back you up to show you that I get it. And I love you and Nash. And—"

She pressed fingers against his mouth, hushing him. "I know," she said.

The crushing tension in his chest eased. "You do?"

"Yeah. That's why I'm here. To tell you. I'm sorry, Tucker."

"Sorry? For what?"

"For not listening. For not giving you a chance. For runnin' away. Don told me about the contract. And I read the note on the flowers."

"Flowers?"

"Yeah. But why didn't you deliver 'em in person?"

His brain felt like a dog chasing its tail. "I…ah…see…" He huffed out a breath. "I heard you talking to those jerks from Midnight Records. So I…well, when you ignored me, I dumped the flowers in the trash and left."

Her look of confusion returned. "Then how did Don get them?"

Yeah, how *did* Dandy Don get the bouquet? Deke's smug expression earlier now made sense. And so did Don's call. "Someone played Cupid." He dropped down on one knee. "What about it, Zoe Parker? Will you let me be the hero in your story?"

"Absolutely!"

He was on his feet instantly, wrapping her in his arms and lifting her. "Where's Nash?" he mumbled against her lips as he kissed her.

"With Rosemary."

"Good." And it was a good thing he was so good at multitasking. His mouth was very busy kissing her as he scooped her into his arms and all but ran to his front door and bumped it open. Zoe snagged the door as he carried her inside and slammed it shut behind them. "Lock it," he growled.

She laughed, the sound breathless, which fanned what had been his slow, steady arousal into something resembling a bonfire. Upstairs in the master suite, he set her down on the bed and dropped to his knees. He snatched the velvet box from the nightstand, opened it and pulled out the diamond engagement ring. "I want to marry you. If you'll let me, I want to be a father to Nash. I love you both more than I've ever loved anyone or anything. Please marry me, Zoe."

"Yes," she breathed.

He slipped the ring on her finger and gathered her close, kissing and stroking her with an intensity he'd never felt before meeting her.

She gulped and stuttered, "W-what are you doing, Tucker?"

"I'm making love to Bent Star's newest singing sensation and the woman soon to be my wife."

She melted in his arms and the kiss deepened as her mouth sucked greedily at his. The taste of her, the very essence of her seeped into him, filling up an emptiness he'd never acknowledged. Desperate for her, he wasn't very careful as he tore at her clothes, then his own. Her skin flushed rosy as he skimmed his hands across her, cupping her breasts and testing the warmth between her thighs. Zoe's breath hitched as she moaned, a husky sound of approval. Her hips arched in a demanding invitation. He managed to put on the condom—barely—and slid inside. He'd come home at last. They moved together, and she trembled beneath him. He tried to stay gentle, but the need for her overcame everything as he plunged in and out. She met each of his thrusts until both of them were panting.

Zoe clenched around him, going stiff when her release burst around him. He followed her over the edge, seeing stars dancing across his vision. He lay over her, weighing her down, knowing he needed to shift off her so they both could breathe. Then he heard voices coming through the open window.

"I'm tellin' you, big brother, the bumper sticker says if this RV is rockin', don't bother knockin'."

Dillon. And from the sound of the laughter in response, Deke. He was going to kill his brothers. Kill them dead and tell his mother they died in their sleep. Zoe shook under him as he stared at her. Her eyes were squeezed shut, and he worried that she was upset and about to cry. Then laughter burst out of her.

"Good thing we came inside, huh?" she managed to say around her giggles.

He laughed too, but the option of killing his brothers remained on the table.

"I love you, angel."

She raised her head and kissed him. "You still want to be my hero?"

"Absolutely," he vowed.

Epilogue

The gazebo in the backyard of Katherine's home was bedecked with flowers touched by the last golden rays of the setting sun. The clouds decorating the western sky blazed with brilliant colors, a picture postcard background as Judge Nelligan, Tucker and Chase waited for the bride. Family and friends sat on rows of white wooden chairs. Deacon, Dillon and the Sons of Nashville sat off to one side, providing the music. Keisha came down the aisle between the chairs, carrying Nash, who was trying to eat the flowers of the boutonniere pinned to the lapel of his miniature tuxedo.

Zoe appeared on Don Easley's arm, and Tucker remembered to breathe when Chase elbowed him in the back. His bride was…beautiful. Her wedding dress was the exact opposite of the one she'd worn the first time he saw her. Made of heavy lace, it clung to her curves, but the skirt was just full enough to make walking down the aisle and stepping into the gazebo easy. She wore boots with stitching to match the lace of her dress, a white Stetson with lace, flowers and a veil. His mother's pearls, the same strand Quin had worn when she married Deacon, circled Zoe's neck. And her smile lit up the countryside. Tucker was captivated.

The judge offered their vows and they dutifully recited them. Tucker added a diamond-covered band to the engagement ring on Zoe's finger. She placed a platinum band on his. Before Judge Nelligan pronounced them husband and wife, the Sons began to play. After a soft piano opening played by Dillon, Deke sang. "This is the day, when I give you my heart. Knowing we're together, knowing we'll never part. All I can see is you standing there, seeing in your eyes the love that we share. And then it comes over me. This is the way it should be. Now and forever, my life is with you."

"My newest song," Zoe whispered, her eyes misty. "For you."

"You may kiss your bride," the judge announced. Tucker did. Thoroughly. He took her into his arms, bent her back over his arm and kissed her deeply. Righting Zoe, he reached for Nash. He held his son easily in one arm with his wife gathered under his other. Tucker Tate was a man who knew where he was going. His life was exactly on track—and he was precisely where he wanted to be.

* * * * *

Don't miss any of these cowgirl romances
from Silver James

Cowgirls Don't Cry
The Cowgirl's Little Secret
The Boss and His Cowgirl
Convenient Cowgirl Bride
Redeemed by the Cowgirl
Claiming the Cowgirl's Baby
The Cowboy's Christmas Proposition
Billionaire Country

Available now from Harlequin Desire!

SPECIAL EXCERPT FROM

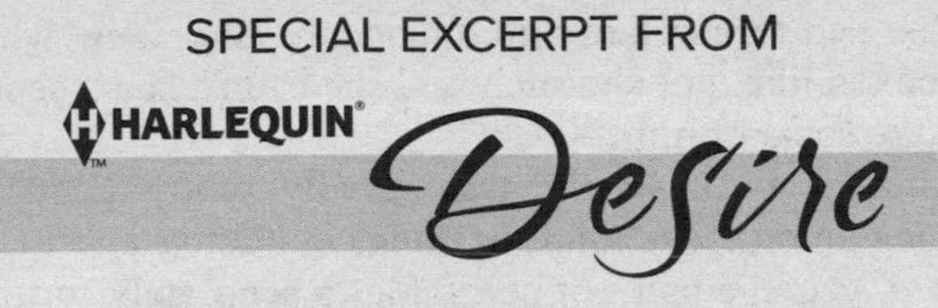

Unfairly labeled by his family's dark reputation, brooding rancher Levi Tucker is done playing by the rules. He demands a new mansion designed by famous architect Faith Grayson, an innocent beauty he would only corrupt...but he must *have her.*

Read on for a sneak peek at
Need Me, Cowboy
by New York Times *bestselling author Maisey Yates!*

Faith had designed buildings that had changed skylines, and she'd done homes for the rich and the famous.

Levi Tucker was something else. He was infamous.

The self-made millionaire who had spent the past five years in prison and was now digging his way back…

He wanted her. And yeah, it interested her.

She let out a long, slow breath as she rounded the final curve on the mountain driveway, the vacant lot coming into view. But it wasn't the lot, or the scenery surrounding it, that stood out in her vision first and foremost. No, it was the man, with his hands shoved into the pockets of his battered jeans, worn cowboy boots on his feet. He had on a black T-shirt, in spite of the morning chill, and a black cowboy hat was pressed firmly on his head.

HDEXP0319

She had researched him, obviously. She knew what he looked like, but she supposed she hadn't had a sense of…the scale of him.

Strange, because she was usually pretty good at picking up on those kinds of things in photographs.

And yet, she had not been able to accurately form a picture of the man in her mind. And when she got out of the car, she was struck by the way he seemed to fill this vast, empty space.

That also didn't make any sense.

He was big. Over six feet and with broad shoulders, but he didn't fill this space. Not literally.

But she could feel his presence as soon as the cold air wrapped itself around her body upon exiting the car.

And when his ice-blue eyes connected with hers, she drew in a breath. She was certain he filled her lungs, too.

Because that air no longer felt cold. It felt hot. Impossibly so.

Because those blue eyes burned with something.

Rage. Anger.

Not at her—in fact, his expression seemed almost friendly.

But there was something simmering beneath the surface…and it had touched her already.

HDEXP0319

Love Harlequin romance?

DISCOVER.

Be the first to find out about promotions, news and exclusive content!

Facebook.com/HarlequinBooks

Twitter.com/HarlequinBooks

Instagram.com/HarlequinBooks

Pinterest.com/HarlequinBooks

ReaderService.com

EXPLORE.

Sign up for the Harlequin e-newsletter and download a free book from any series at **TryHarlequin.com.**

CONNECT.

Join our Harlequin community to share your thoughts and connect with other romance readers!

Facebook.com/groups/HarlequinConnection

ROMANCE WHEN YOU NEED IT

HSOCIAL2018